Laure
half the
audience gasped

as Dash pulled off his shirt, revealing his well-toned torso.

"Are we really the same?" Dash asked, directing his question to Lauren. "If we are, then interview me without being embarrassed. Or take off your clothes and I'll interview you! I'm a reporter, too, you know."

Lauren stared dumbstruck.

"What's the matter?" Dash teased her. "You're saying that men don't have the right to privacy, so this shouldn't bother you." He started to unbuckle his belt.

"Take it all off!" a girl in the audience shouted.

"Come on," Dash said, walking toward Lauren and grabbing her hands. "Let's strip together, and show the world we're exactly alike."

A wrenching sob burst from Lauren's throat, and tears spilled from her eyes. Tearing her hands out of Dash's, she ran out of the room.

Don't miss these books
in the exciting FRESHMAN DORM
series

FRESHMAN FLAMES

LINDA A. COONEY

HarperPaperbacks
A Division of HarperCollinsPublishers

If you purchased this book without a cover, you should be aware that this book is stolen property. It was reported as "unsold and destroyed" to the publisher and neither the author nor the publisher has received any payment for this "stripped book."

This is a work of fiction. The characters, incidents, and dialogues are products of the author's imagination and are not to be construed as real. Any resemblance to actual events or persons, living or dead, is entirely coincidental.

HarperPaperbacks   *A Division of* HarperCollins*Publishers*
10 East 53rd Street, New York, N.Y. 10022

Copyright © 1991 by Linda Alper and Kevin Cooney
All rights reserved. No part of this book may be used or reproduced in any manner whatsoever without written permission of the publisher, except in the case of brief quotations embodied in critical articles and reviews. For information address HarperCollins*Publishers,*
10 East 53rd Street, New York, N.Y. 10022.

Cover art by Tony Greco

First printing: October 1991

Printed in the United States of America

HarperPaperbacks and colophon are trademarks of HarperCollins*Publishers*

10 9 8 7 6 5 4 3 2 1

One

....

"I know this is supposed to be a breakfast meeting," Lauren Turnbell-Smythe said to Dash Ramirez as they walked across the University of Springfield dorm green Sunday morning, "but I won't be able to eat a thing. I'm too nervous!"

"Why?" Dash asked as he sauntered beside Lauren in his high-top sneakers. "It's just the same people we see in the newspaper office every day." He poked her in the side. "Besides, I'm sure you'll have the best table manners of anyone there."

Lauren stopped walking and took a deep breath of the cool, pine-scented breeze blowing down off the distant mountaintops. She closed her eyes, letting the warmth of the sun bathe her face. Dash was right: there was nothing to be nervous about. If anything, she knew she should feel excited. After several months of contributing articles to the U of S *Weekly Journal*, she'd finally been invited to be an official member of the staff. At this very moment, she was on her way to her first Sunday breakfast meeting for *Journal* staffers at the University Café. She'd finally made it; she was in. So why did her legs feel so shaky?

Lauren felt a gentle pressure on her lips. Opening her eyes, she saw Dash's long lashes inches from hers as he kissed her softly. His fingers intertwined with hers as he pulled her to him. Lauren tried to lose herself in Dash's embrace, feeling him wrapped around her like a protective shield.

"Is that better?" Dash asked.

Lauren looked up at her boyfriend through her wire-rimmed glasses. Dash was tall and lean, with a sculpted face and olive skin. His thick, black hair was half-hidden beneath a red bandanna tied across his forehead. He wore a black T-shirt, olive drab army pants, and the usual few days' growth of black stubble on his cheeks.

He looked like a street-wise kid from a not-so-safe neighborhood, but Lauren had learned this was just a disguise. Dash's father was president of a bank, and his M.B.A. mother was a hospital administrator. But if Dash wanted to hide his upper middle class background, that was fine with Lauren. Everything Dash did was fine with Lauren.

"I know I'm acting silly," Lauren admitted. "And it's really not the breakfast that I'm worried about. It's living up to my potential. We've written a few good articles together, but what if that was just a fluke? What if I'm really not talented after all? I don't want Greg to think he made a big mistake by choosing me." Greg Sukamaki was editor-in-chief of the *Journal*.

"Greg knew exactly what he was doing," Dash said firmly. "You're a terrific writer. You really dig down into the heart of things. Why do you think our pieces were so good?"

"I thought maybe it was you," Lauren admitted as they began walking again, hand in hand. "After all, you're a junior and more experienced than I am, not to mention an assistant editor."

"It was a *team effort*," Dash emphasized. "I never could have done it without you. And everybody at the paper knows that."

"We *do* make a good team, don't we?" Lauren asked.

"And not just at the paper," Dash said, wrapping his arm around her waist and nuzzling her earlobe.

Lauren relaxed against Dash as they approached

the old library, a four-story stone building which was now used as the Student Activities center. Lauren followed Dash down the dark, stone staircase leading to the University Café in the basement. The café was cool and dark. A former reading room, its walls were still lined with old, wooden bookshelves filled with dusty, leather-bound volumes. Fluorescent lights and hanging plants brightened up the place.

Trying not to feel self-conscious, Lauren trailed Dash to the back table, already filled with familiar faces. Greg Sukamaki sat at the head of the table talking to Alison Argonbright, an investigative journalist. Lauren also recognized Charlie Mandelkern, the sports reporter, and Richard Levine, who wrote a column with Alison.

"Dash! Lauren!" Greg called, waving them over. "I'm glad you're here. Hurry up and order breakfast so we can get started. We have a lot on the agenda this morning."

"You're always telling us what to do," Dash jibed, shaking his head as he pulled out an empty chair for Lauren. "Who made you boss?"

Lauren eyed Dash enviously as she sat down. Never in a million years could Lauren have joked around that way with her editor-in-chief. But that was the difference between Dash and her—Dash was comfortable with people. Lauren wished she could feel as free and easy, but she was always worrying that she was being too forward or hurting someone's feelings.

"Let's get down to business," Greg said, after Dash and Lauren had placed their breakfast orders. He rose from the table. "First of all, I'd like to welcome Lauren Turnbell-Smythe to the *Weekly Journal* staff. I'm sure most of you already know her from her collaboration with Dash Ramirez on the attempted destruction of Bickford Lane, their three-part series on recycling, and their exposé on fraternity hazing."

"Not bad for a freshman!" shouted Alison Argonbright.

"Yeah," agreed Ellen Greenfield, production editor for the paper. "You helped make an honest man of Dash. Before you got here, all he did was stink up the office with his cigarettes."

"You've definitely added class to this group of goons," Dash agreed. "Now I finally have someone to work with who's on my own intellectual level."

Embarrassed by all the attention, Lauren ran her finger along the lacework of names carved into the surface of the thick, wooden table.

"You'd better get used to this," Ellen warned her. "It only gets worse."

"And speaking of the hazing article," Greg continued, "I have an important announcement to make. Our newest staffer and her intellectual colleague are the winners of this year's University

Regents' Award for Best Investigative Reporting."

Everyone around the table applauded, and someone shouted, "Way to go!"

Dash whooped with delight and threw his arms around Lauren. "We did it!" he cried. "I told you we're a winning combination!"

Lauren looked at Dash in confusion. "I don't get it," she said. "What is . . .?"

"Let me quote the board of judges," Greg said, reading from a piece of paper on his clipboard. "'Ramirez and Turnbell-Smythe did a masterful job uncovering the barbaric practices of Omega Delta Tau. The piece was well-researched, well-written, and upheld the highest standards of investigative reporting: to inform, to outrage, and to effect change.'"

Lauren felt a burst of adrenaline as she remembered how scared she'd been to hide in the bushes outside the ODT house one night during last semester's rush. On a tip from her friend, KC Angeletti, Lauren had learned that some of the ODTs were planning to haze an awkward, skinny freshman whom they didn't want to join their fraternity. The frat boys had gotten Howard Benmann dangerously drunk, then locked him in the trunk of a car. Howard might have suffocated if Lauren hadn't jumped out of the bushes at that moment and screamed at the top of her lungs. Lauren had frightened the ODTs away, rescued

Howard and, with Dash, had written a story that had the campus talking for weeks.

"It's the highest award they give to journalists at this university," Dash explained. "And they only give out one award per year. It's an incredible honor."

The meaning of it all was finally beginning to sink in. In less than a year, Lauren had gone from someone who was almost too scared to enter the newspaper office and ask for a writing assignment, to a full-fledged, award-winning journalist! Lauren screamed and threw her arms around Dash's neck. "I can't believe it!" she cried. "I've never won anything in my life!"

"This is just the beginning," Dash said confidently. "There's no reason why we can't win it again next year."

"Hey!" said Richard Levine. "Give the rest of us a chance."

"Congratulations to both of you," Greg said, making a checkmark on his list. "Next item, work in progress. I'd like each of you to tell me what you're doing, how far you've come, and when I can expect it on my desk." He turned to Lauren and Dash. "Not to dominate this morning's meeting with Turnbell-Smythe and Ramirez, but, through a weird twist of fate, it turns out the two of them will be exploring opposite sides of the same issue—a somewhat controversial issue—and

I'd like to get your input. Lauren, you want to give us a preview?" Greg sat down.

Lauren felt the excitement drain from her body, quickly replaced with dread. Fifteen pairs of eyes stared at her. It would be hard enough to work on her next assignment, but she hadn't realized she'd have to talk about it in front of other people. That's why she'd become a writer in the first place, so she could hide behind her words, without having to be seen or heard.

"Up on your feet, Lauren," Greg said. "Don't be bashful."

"Hey!" Dash said, rising to Lauren's defense. "Give her a chance. She doesn't have to jump every time you snap your fingers. Take your time, Lauren."

With a grateful look at Dash, Lauren hesitantly rose from her chair. "I'm writing about sex discrimination," she said quietly, her voice hoarse.

"Louder!" Alison Argonbright called from down the table.

Lauren cleared her throat. "Sex discrimination means denying someone certain rights or privileges because of their gender. Usually that means women aren't allowed to do all the things men can do."

Lauren's voice was shaking, but she forced herself to continue, bolstered by Dash's encouraging gaze. "Last week, I was a victim of sex discrimination. I tried to cover the volleyball team's winning streak for the paper, but when I went into the men's locker room to interview the players, Coach Brandes kicked me out because I'm a woman."

Lauren noticed that her fingers were starting to hurt. Looking down at her hands, she realized that she'd been digging her thumbnails into the soft flesh at the tips of her fingers, leaving dark-red, crescent-shaped marks.

"You're doing fine," Dash whispered. "Keep going."

Lauren spread her fingers flat on the table and took a deep breath. "The worst part," she said, "is that all the men's coaches must have told their players not to talk to me, because none of the male jocks will give me an interview now. It's like they're a closed society, or they have something against women reporters. I'm not going to give up, though. No matter what it takes, I'm going to line up some interviews and prove that female reporters have just as much right to enter the men's locker rooms as male reporters do. Uh . . . that's it," Lauren finished, sinking weakly into her chair.

People around the table were nodding, and Dash gave her the thumbs-up sign. Maybe she hadn't done so badly after all.

"Dash?" Greg said.

Dash hopped up and flashed his sexy grin. "I guess we've stirred up some pretty strong feelings," he said. "Equality is a big deal, and I wouldn't think of denying anyone his or her rights just because of gender."

"He's my kind of guy," Ellen Greenfield called out.

"Of course," Dash continued, with a twinkle in his eye, "equality works both ways. If a female reporter should be allowed in the men's locker room, then it's only logical to conclude that a male reporter should be allowed in the women's locker room."

"Oooh! I'm for that!" said Charlie Mandelkern. "Have you seen the bodies on the women's swim team? I'd sure like to get a closer look!"

"You're disgusting, Charlie," Ellen said, slapping him on the arm.

Dash focused his smoldering, dark eyes on Ellen. "Suddenly equality doesn't seem like such a great idea, does it?" he asked.

"This is different . . ." Ellen began.

"What's different about it?" Dash asked, propping one sneakered foot on his chair, and leaning an elbow on one knee. "Are you saying male reporters can't be objective about the nude human form, but females can?"

"Guys are leches," Alison said.

Dash's eyebrows raised in mock dismay. "That's

so sexist! And maybe it's simply because men have been banned from women's locker rooms, denied the opportunity to *see* the naked female body, to get *comfortable* with it that—"

"Dash!" Lauren said in alarm.

Dash laughed. "So much for equality," he concluded. "I haven't begun my research yet, but I have no doubt I'll be able to prove that your "equality" argument is a crock. If women object to having men in their locker room, then you can't blame men for feeling the same way." Slinging his leg over his chair, Dash straddled it and grinned impishly.

Lauren felt her face grow hot with embarrassment. It had been hard enough standing up in front of all these people, but Dash, without even trying, had practically destroyed her argument. The worst part was that he didn't even *care* about this issue. For him, it was all a joke.

"Moving on," Greg said.

While the rest of the reporters described their assignments, Lauren nibbled at the dry whole wheat toast which the waitress had deposited in front of her. What little confidence she'd had was completely shattered.

"You're dismissed," Greg said at the end of the hour, draining the last of his coffee with a slurp. "Lauren, Dash, stay a minute. I need to talk to you."

As the rest of the *Journal* staffers paid their bills and filed out of the basement café, Greg got up from his chair and moved down the table to sit closer to them.

"First of all," Greg said, "I hope you have some nice clothes, because the University Regents banquet is two weeks from yesterday. That's where you'll accept your award. You also might want to prepare a short acceptance speech."

"Wow!" Lauren said. "It sounds like the Academy Awards."

"I'd like to thank my mother, my father, my agent . . ." Dash joked, making his voice echo as if speaking into a microphone.

"Hey!" Lauren chided him. "Don't forget about me."

"Not possible," Dash said, scooting his chair closer to her and putting his arm around her shoulder. "I'd be nowhere without you."

Lauren breathed in Dash's clean fragrance of lemon and soap and she felt her body relax. Maybe she'd let herself get too defensive about this locker room story. It wasn't right to resent Dash just because he felt more comfortable with himself than she did.

"The other thing I wanted to ask you," Greg continued, "was if you'd be interested in debating your issue at the student union, a week from Wednesday. It's a monthly forum, and it's open to everyone. The guy who organizes it, Thornton Lewis, is a friend of mine, and I suggested your story to him since it seems pretty topical right now."

"Sounds like fun," Dash said. "We'll have our arguments down by then, so it shouldn't be a big deal. What do you say, Lauren?"

"Debate?" Lauren whispered to Greg. "You mean go up in front of a group of people?"

Greg nodded. "It's not a big crowd. These intellectual battles don't pull as many people as two meathead football teams trying to knock each other down. Only about a hundred people usually show up."

It didn't matter whether Greg had said a hundred or a thousand. To Lauren, it sounded equally impossible. She hadn't even felt comfortable talking today to fifteen people she already knew. Lauren was certain that if she dared to go up on stage, her palms would sweat, her voice would quiver, and her brain would shut down in terror. There was no way she'd be able to remember her own name, let alone make a coherent argument.

"Well?" Greg asked. "What should I tell Thornton?"

"I don't know," Lauren said hesitantly. While the last thing she felt like doing was debating in public, she couldn't bring herself to say no. It wasn't that she was worried Greg or Dash would think less of her; it was much bigger than that. Saying no would be giving in to her fears. It would be taking a giant step backward.

Lauren had come so far this year, not only by succeeding at the *Journal*, but by standing up for herself, by becoming the person she wanted to be. Lauren had arrived at the U of S a pampered rich girl, dressed in expensive cashmere and tweeds, who'd always done exactly what her mother told her. Little by little, though, she'd struggled for independence. She'd refused to join her mother's exclusive sorority, Tri Beta, even though it had meant her mother cut her off without a cent. Lauren had learned to support herself financially, working as a maid at the Springfield Mountain Inn, and had even moved to a grim, off-campus apartment to save money. While each step had been difficult, Lauren ended up feeling better about herself, stronger.

The same held true for the locker room story, though this time Lauren had had some help. Lauren had been afraid to enter the men's locker room to interview the volleyball players, and might never have dared to if Liza Ruff hadn't literally pushed her through the door.

Liza Ruff, a nervy, brassy freshman, had bought Lauren's dorm contract. The two had become good friends recently, and in the process Liza had helped Lauren overcome some of her shyness. *Go for it*, Liza was always saying. *If at first you don't succeed, then knock the door down!*

"Look, Lauren," Dash said, "if you don't want to do this, it's fine with me. I understand if public speaking makes you a little nervous."

"I'll do it," Lauren blurted. "Just tell me where and when."

Dash looked surprised, but pleased. "May the best man win!" he said. "Or woman." He planted a kiss on Lauren's cheek.

Now that Lauren had made a decision, she felt her confidence return. "No matter who wins," she said, "let's treat ourselves to a victory celebration afterward." She smiled at Dash lovingly.

Greg stood up. "I hope you guys still feel this lovey dovey *after* the debate," he said. "There might be hard feelings, you know."

"Not on my part," Dash said. "I don't really care about this issue. I'm just doing it for fun."

"And I'm doing it to prove I can," Lauren said.

Greg nodded and picked up his clipboard. "Good," he said. "Just make sure your articles are on my desk a week from tomorrow. I want to publish them right after the debate." Greg left some money on the table, and headed for the exit.

Dash, too, took some cash from his wallet, enough to pay for Lauren and himself. "It's a gorgeous day," he said. "Let's go for a walk."

Lauren stopped his hand as he laid the money

down. "You don't have to pay for me," she said. "I can handle it."

"I want to," Dash said. "And I'm not being sexist. I just want to celebrate the fact that you're a full-timer. Now we'll have an excuse to spend even more time together."

"If we still want to after the debate," Lauren said quietly.

Dash gave her a puzzled look. "What are you talking about? You didn't really take Greg seriously, did you?"

Lauren shrugged. "Not really, but I *did* feel some resentment when you were talking about your side of the argument. It all seemed so *easy* for you, so effortless. And it made me jealous. I'm afraid the same thing might happen when we debate."

"It won't," Dash said, "because by the time you get up there at the student union, you're going to be so well-versed in your arguments, so well-rehearsed, that I'm going to have to struggle just to get anybody to listen to me."

"The only way that would ever happen is if you waved a magic wand," Lauren said.

"I can do better than that," Dash said. "I can work with you. Help you. And you can help me, too. There's no rule that says we can't collaborate on this assignment. You'll tell me your arguments, I'll tell you mine, and that will help us prepare our rebuttals."

Lauren slowly rose from her chair. "Is that legal? I mean, isn't it supposed to be more of an ad lib thing, where we're thinking on our feet?"

"Not at all," Dash said, leaping from his chair and grabbing Lauren's hand. "Those political debates you see on television are all scripted. You don't think a candidate's going to go up there without knowing all the questions and answers in advance, do you?"

"I guess you're right," Lauren said as Dash led her up the stairs. "But I don't want this to be a one-sided thing where you're giving me all the help and advice."

"I believe in equality, remember" Dash said. "I'll take any help you have to offer."

"I've already thought of something," Lauren said as they re-emerged onto the dorm green. Lauren could hear the distant whine of a lawnmower, and the warm air carried the smell of cut grass. "This coming Friday, Winnie, Faith, KC, and a bunch of other friends are going to watch videos in the basement of Forest Hall. Winnie's roommate, Melissa McDormand, will be there. She's a middle-distance runner on the track team. Why don't you come with me and interview her?"

"Great idea!" Dash said. "I wasn't planning to spend Friday night without you, anyway."

Lauren stopped walking and planted herself in

front of Dash. "I'm glad we can work together, even if we are on opposing sides," she said. "I'll bet another couple might have gotten into an argument over this."

"Not us," Dash said, slipping his hands around Lauren's waist. He pulled her closer and kissed her softly on the lips. "Let's leave the *real* battle of the sexes to someone else."

Two
······················

Liza Ruff pulled down the hem of her kelly-green, puckered, stretch mini-dress and pulled up at the neckline which was cut a bit too low. Then she adjusted her hat with the plastic cherries so that the black veil discreetly covered her powder-pale face. For the first time in the months she'd been at U of S, she was entering the dining commons as part of a group, and she wanted to fit in.

"So what did you think of the meeting?" Liza asked her roommate, Faith Crowley, as they got on line to get their meal cards checked. The sounds of murmuring voices, clattering dishes, and clinking silverware rose up from the tables and died before reaching the ceiling of the cavernous hall. Liza had to shout to make herself heard. "I thought it was great that they only invited women to get *our* perspective on coed living. Although, frankly, after living in Langston, I'm just so greatful to have men around that I don't have any complaints."

Liza had started at U of S in the middle of the year, so she hadn't been able to choose her dorm like most of the other freshmen. She'd been stuck, for a few months, in Langston House, an all-female single-room study dorm with a twenty-four-hour quiet rule. Liza had thought she was going to go nuts there. She couldn't vocalize or play her show tunes or practice her tap dancing.

Her career as a future superstar might have been stuck on hold forever if Lauren hadn't sold Liza her dorm contract in Coleridge Hall. Coleridge housed all the performing arts majors, which was what Liza planned to be.

Even better, living in Coleridge meant she'd have a roommate, a built-in friend who shared some of the same interests. So far, though, all of Liza's attempts to befriend Faith had failed. Liza didn't let this get her down.

"Faith!" Liza sang in her brassy voice.

"Hmmm?" Faith asked, barely listening. She stood a little distance away from Liza, and her two best friends from high school, Winnie Gottlieb and KC Angeletti. As usual, she was dressed like a ranch hand in a faded, blue denim blouse, snug blue jeans, and scuffed, black cowboy boots. Her suede, fringed jacket was draped over one arm and her honey-blond hair was pulled back in a neat french braid.

"What's *your* opinion on coed living?" Liza asked. "You didn't say much at the meeting."

"Oh." Faith shrugged. "I'm just glad we have separate floors in Coleridge. I'm also glad we don't have to share bathrooms. Have you seen the guys' bathroom downstairs? It's a mess!"

Liza felt encouraged. Faith had actually said five sentences to her, if you counted "Oh." This was progress. If Liza said something else, it might actually count as a conversation.

"I don't think sharing a bathroom with guys sounds bad at all," Liza said, rolling her blue eyes. "Think how lucky Winnie is. She gets to share her floor *and* a bathroom with all those cute jocks. Can you imagine seeing a constant stream of barechested men in towels parading up and down the hall? That's my idea of heaven."

"It's not as great as you think," Winnie said, bounding up to them on her rubber-soled sneakers and taking her place in line behind them. "They're usually fully dressed, drunk, and hurling objects down the hall at each other. It's more like dodgeball than a parade."

Winnie's short, spikey, brown hair waggled as she talked. She was always full of nervous energy. Even her clothes were vibrant. Today she was wearing a neon green tank top with hot pink lycra tights and purple socks. Dangling from her right earlobe was a yellow feather, and from her left, a pair of clear red dice, which clacked against each other every time she turned her head.

"That's why I prefer the peace and quiet of Langston House," KC said, putting down her leather briefcase so she could search for her meal card in her purse. "I can walk down the hall without wearing a crash helmet, and I don't have to worry about looking good just to use the bathroom."

Unlike Liza, Faith, and Winnie, KC preferred conservative clothes. Today she was wearing a no-nonsense, gray wool suit and black pumps. The only good thing Liza could say about the suit was that it brought out the gray of KC's large, thick-lashed eyes. Liza understood that KC wanted to be president of a major corporation someday, and that she was dressing the part, but it seemed like such a waste of a good figure. KC was still a knockout, though, with long, dark hair framing her beautiful face.

After they'd checked their cards at the desk, Liza followed Faith into the kitchen. Little by little, she planned to break down Faith's resistance.

"So what did you think of that 'Snatch Breakfast' idea?" Liza asked Faith as they grabbed their silverware from the plastic bins. At the dorm meeting, it had been announced that a week from Sunday, all the girls could snatch a dorm guy out of bed and drag him to the dining commons.

Faith paused in front of the dessert racks which, for some reason, were the first item on the dinner line, and selected vanilla pudding. "There's no one I really want to snatch," she said. "But I guess it'll be fun for some people."

"Like me!" Winnie said, spinning on her rubber soles and balancing her empty tray on her head. "I'm going to dress up as a cavewoman, club Josh over the head, and drag him to breakfast by his hair." Josh Gaffey, Winnie's boyfriend, was a computer major who lived on the same floor as Winnie in Forest Hall.

"Go for it!" Liza said. "If I had a boyfriend, I'd do the same thing—even if there wasn't a snatch breakfast." Liza grabbed two plates of giant chocolate chip cookies, then slid her tray to the steamy, glass-enclosed entrée section where she ordered one of everything.

"I think I'll use the more subtle approach with Peter," KC said. "He's such a heavy sleeper, I'll probably have to use a foghorn to wake him up."

"Honey," Liza drawled, "if I looked like you, I

wouldn't need to do *anything* to get a man's attention. He'll probably stay up all night just waiting for you to knock on his door."

KC gave Liza a grateful smile. "I know you're exaggerating," she said, "but it's nice to hear. You're certainly good for my ego."

"Yeah," Winnie chimed in. "Stick around!"

Liza smiled triumphantly as the four girls picked up their loaded trays and headed back out to the dining hall. Even if Faith didn't like her, Winnie and KC finally did. For the first time in her life, Liza felt accepted. She'd had a few friends back in New York City, but none of them ever lasted very long.

Maybe it was genetic. Her parents didn't have any friends, either, though in their case it was because they didn't try. They seemed content to come home every evening and sit in front of the television in their drab, little apartment. They never invited anyone over, except for Liza's great Aunt Mathilda who visited once a year from Florida.

Liza loved her parents, but she was afraid she'd become just like them—working at a low-level job, being an anonymous face in the crowd, living and dying without the world even noticing. That's why she was determined to make the most of college. And forming lasting friendships was an important part of that. Winnie, KC, and Lauren had been won over, because Liza was willing to listen to their problems, day or night. Liza was sure this approach would work with Faith, too, if only she could figure out what problem it was that Faith needed solved.

The girls found an empty table and sat down.

"You know, Liza," Winnie said, placing a friendly hand on Liza's arm, "I never got a chance to thank you for saving my hotline benefit. If it weren't for you, we would have had to refund all the tickets and the hotline would have been five hundred dollars in the hole. But thanks to you, we made over five thousand dollars!"

When the comedian scheduled to perform at the benefit hadn't shown up, Liza had run back to Coleridge Hall and rounded up over a dozen performers who'd put on an entertaining, if eclectic, show.

"I really didn't do anything," Liza said modestly. "Faith's the one who talked everyone into it."

Faith, who was sitting diagonally across from Liza, looked up in surprise. "I did not," she said. "You did all the talking." Faith turned to Winnie, who sat beside her. "You should have seen Liza," she said, seeming to soften up. "Talk about armtwisting. Liza talked so loud and fast, no one had a chance to say no. And if they had, Liza would probably have lassoed them together and dragged them to Swedenbourg House with her bare hands."

Winnie smiled. "You were also a great emcee, Liza," she said. "You had the audience in stitches. I really owe you. A lot of troubled people out there would thank you, too, if they knew that you helped keep the hotline open."

"Stop thanking me!" Liza said, though she was clearly happy with all the attention. "Let's talk about you, Winnie," she went on, plucking a breadstick from her tray with two long, red fingernails. "What are you planning to do now that the benefit is over?"

Winnie leaned back in her chair and absently stirred her chocolate milk with a clear, plastic straw. "I'm planning to be really mellow," she said. "I want to try to forget that my father ever reappeared in my life, and I want to spend time with Josh and work for the hotline and finish my psych paper. That's about it."

"Sounds good to me," Liza said as she crunched noisily on her breadstick, spraying crumbs all over her lap. "You've been through a really difficult time. If you ever want to talk about anything, my door is open, twenty-four hours a day."

"*Our* door," Faith reminded Liza. "I live there, too."

"Of course. That's what I meant to say," Liza said, reaching into her huge, canvas tote bag. "I've got something you'll really like, Winnie." Liza fished through the tap shoes, dirty tights, sheet music, and makeup until she felt the plastic cylinder. "Here it is," she said, presenting the white, plastic jar. "It's Felicia Mauler's Sea Mud Cream. You spread it all over your face and let it dry, then rinse with lukewarm water. You'll feel like a new person."

"Thanks!" Winnie said, taking it.

"Let me know if that stuff works," KC said, spearing a fried potato with her fork. "I wouldn't mind being a whole new person, too."

"Why?" Liza asked with interest. "You have a great life! You're in the best sorority on campus, you're a fashion model, and you've got a really nice boyfriend."

KC put her fork down and picked up her paper napkin. "It's not that there's anything wrong," she said, tearing a narrow strip off the napkin. "It's just that there's too much of it right now." KC tore another strip from the napkin. "I'm always moving at high speed, just to fit everything in, and I'm always worrying about money. Even with the modeling, I still don't have enough to afford tutoring, clothes, and my sorority dues. It's making me really anxious." KC's napkin was now completely shredded.

"Just slow down," Liza counseled. "Or you'll burn yourself out."

"I know," KC said. "The worst part is, I've finally figured out what's most important in my life, but I haven't done anything about it. Maybe I'm keeping myself busy just so I have an excuse for running away from him."

"Peter?" Liza asked. Peter Dvorsky, KC's boyfriend, was a sophomore photography major who lived on the first floor of Liza's dorm.

KC nodded, and tucked a strand of her long, brown hair behind her ear. "You know, Liza, you're the one who made me realize how much I need people, and how much I need Peter. I told him that, by the way. But even that wasn't the whole truth. I don't just need him." KC paused and bit her lower lip. Then she looked around her, as if she was afraid someone might overhear. "I love him," she whispered.

"Yay!" Winnie cried, clapping her hands. "I knew you'd realize it eventually."

Faith gasped. "KC! I never thought I'd hear you say those words about anybody! But I'm glad it's Peter."

"So?" Liza asked, slapping her hands down on the table. "Have you told Peter yet?"

"No," KC admitted. "But I want to. I will. When I get up the nerve."

"What is there to be nervous about?" Liza demanded. "He feels the same way about you, right?"

"I'm not sure," KC said. "I mean, I know he likes me . . . I'd even say he cares about me . . .

but I can't tell how *I'm* feeling half the time. I certainly couldn't guess what *he's* feeling."

"Well, I can," Liza said with confidence. "Peter's crazy about you; it's obvious from the way he's on cloud nine all the time. All you have to do is open your mouth and say you love him. I guarantee you'll hear him say the same thing back to you."

"Do you really think so?" KC asked.

"Cross my heart," Liza assured her. "He's a goner for sure. So what are you waiting for? Go ahead. Jump in. Start the rest of your life! Wait a minute . . ." Liza began fishing in her tote bag again. "I've got something I want you to read. One of the volleyball players recommended it when Lauren and I were in their locker room." Liza pulled out a hardcover book, titled *Brain Power: Winning's All in Your Head*. "It teaches you to think positively and go for what you want."

"Thanks!" KC said, taking it. "That's the philosophy I try to live by."

"Gee, Mr. Wizard," Faith said, half-wistfully. "Is there anything in that black bag for me?"

Liza looked over at Faith. Here was her chance. Faith had never asked her for anything, nor had Faith ever taken anything from Liza, even when Liza had made a friendly offer. Most of the time, Faith avoided their room altogether.

"What do you want?" Liza asked eagerly. "I'm

sure I can find it in my bag of tricks."

"I doubt it," Faith said, turning her head away and staring out the ceiling-high window that framed the distant mountaintops.

"Give me a hint," Liza insisted.

Faith shrugged. "I don't even know myself," she said. "Maybe I don't want anything." She heaved a deep sigh.

"You don't sound too happy," Liza observed. "There's got to be something that would make your life better."

"I doubt it."

"Sure there is," Liza pressed on. "We just need to figure out what it is. Why don't I start mentioning things, and you can say yes or no. Clothes?"

"No."

"Money?"

"No."

"Fame? That would do it for me."

Faith fixed her brown eyes on Liza. "Actually, *anything* would make my life better. Or at least more interesting. Right now I've got to be the most boring person on the planet."

"Oh, come on," said Winnie. "How many freshmen get to direct shows, have a fling with a gorgeous frat guy, and get romanced by one of America's hottest movie stars? I'd say your life is anything but dull."

"No," Faith insisted. "I'm boring. Boring and bored. I'm not working on any projects for the theater department, and I just finished two major papers and pulled an A and an A-. I even did well on my calculus test, mainly because I had nothing else to do but study for it."

"That doesn't sound too bad to me," KC commented. "I'd give anything to get grades like that."

"And I'd give anything to have a life that's as exciting and well-rounded as yours," Faith said to KC. "You don't just go to school. You have a career *and* a boyfriend. You too, Winnie. I'm just an anonymous freshman. Sweet, maternal, good girl Faith. And the only one of us who doesn't have a steady boyfriend. I'm tired of being a fifth wheel around all you happy couples."

"I don't have a boyfriend," Liza said, ignoring the fact that Faith hadn't included her in the term 'us.' It didn't matter, anyway. Faith had finally given Liza something to work toward. At last there was something Liza could do to help. "I'll find someone for you," Liza volunteered, flapping her red-nailed fingers. "I'm a born matchmaker. It's in my blood! My great-grandmother back in Russia did it for a living."

"Please don't worry about it," Faith said

anxiously. "It's not your problem."

"It is now!" Liza crowed. "You want excitement and romance? You've got it! Just leave it to me!"

Three

························

"I think I can tell him. I know I can tell him. I think I can tell him. I know I can tell him," KC chanted to herself as she marched across the dorm green toward Coleridge Hall. KC had stayed up all night reading the book Liza lent her, and she'd been inspired by the book's motto: *I think I can win. I know I can win.*

KC had modified the motto for her own use, but the basic idea was the same. And if it worked for the volleyball team, which had now won seventeen straight victories, it had to work for a college freshman who was merely hoping to say three little words without being rejected.

Besides, this philosophy was merely restating what KC had believed all her life. If you set your mind to something, and believed in yourself strongly enough, you could accomplish anything.

She hoped.

As KC approached Coleridge Hall, she could hear opera music coming from an open window on the second floor, as well as the plaintive strains of someone playing scales on a violin.

Pushing open the door to the dorm, KC turned left, heading for the janitor's closet that had been converted into a darkroom. Peter was almost always there, except when he was eating, sleeping, or in class. KC knocked on the door.

"Hold on a minute," Peter's voice came from inside. "I'm fixing a picture."

Peter opened the door a moment later, and the vinegary smell of photographic chemicals wafted out into the hallway. He looked comfortable in his gray sweatshirt and matching sweatpants with the hole in the knee. His hair, a shade somewhere between blond and brown, was cut in no particular style. His face was attractive, though his features were undistinguished.

Sometimes KC had trouble picturing him in her mind when he wasn't around, but she never forgot how she felt about him. She wanted to throw her arms around him, but she couldn't—at least not until she'd said what she came to say.

"Hi," KC said shyly. "Am I interrupting anything?"

"Uh, no, not really." Peter stood in the doorway, making it difficult for KC to enter.

"Can I come in?" KC asked.

"Now?" Peter asked, looking back over his shoulder into the darkroom.

"What's the matter?" KC asked. "You hiding a girl in there?" Though her tone was joking, a tiny part of her feared this might be true. He certainly didn't seem eager to have her around.

"The only girl in my life is you," Peter said, kissing her lightly on the forehead. He retreated backward into the narrow room so KC could follow. "I'm just developing some old negatives."

KC wanted to laugh at herself for being so paranoid. It was amazing how your mind could play tricks on you when you started to let feelings take over, but if that was one of the consequences of being in love, KC was prepared to deal with it.

Closing the door behind her, KC entered the tiny space. The only light came from a single red lightbulb clipped to a metal shelf overhead. Two sides of the room were lined with a wooden counter. On the right counter were three plastic developing trays filled with clear liquid, but the left counter was barely visible under a huge pile of large black-and-white photographs. More photos hung above it, clothespinned to a length of twine. KC recognized almost everyone in the photographs, especially since she was in more than half of them. There were close-ups of her face, portraits of her posing as Katharine Hepburn for last year's U of S Classic Calendar, and wide shots of her clowning around in McLaren Plaza on the statue of Derwood C. Brock, founding president of the University.

"What's all this stuff?" KC asked, rummaging through the pile. She knew better than to touch the ones hanging up because they were still wet.

Peter shrugged. "I'm just trying to get organized, see what I've done this past year."

"You've done a lot," KC said, pulling out an action shot of Kimberly Dayton. Kimberly, a freshman dancer, was Faith's and Liza's next door neighbor. In the photo, Kimberly, dressed in a black catsuit and black cape, was flying gracefully through the air, her long legs open in a split. "That's a great shot!" KC exclaimed. "I can't believe you caught her at just the right moment."

Peter, who was dipping a white sheet of paper into the tray nearest the sink, laughed. "I caught her at a lot of moments," he said. "Most of them bad. This was one of the few good ones."

KC continued looking through the stack. There were several of Winnie's roommate, Melissa McDormand, running the 400 meters, and one of her breaking through the finish tape, her lean arms extended above her head in victory. There was one of Melissa's boyfriend, Brooks Baldwin, mountain climbing on The Rock, a huge slab of concrete formed with cracks and crevices, like the side of a mountain. Though his curly, blond hair made him look like a cherub, his legs and arms bulged with strength.

There was even a photo of Josh Gaffey, Winnie's boyfriend, kneeling on the floor, his arm around an odd-looking robot with a square body and a black sphere for a head. The robot was Alphie, Josh's recent invention for the Computer Science fair. Beneath that photo was another of Josh and Alphie, only in this one, Alphie's mechanical arms seemed to be around Josh's neck, in a choke-like embrace.

"This is more than getting organized," KC said, turning back to look at Peter. "This is everything you've ever done! Wait, let me guess. Your photography teacher was so impressed with your work, he's invited you to do an exhibit here on campus, and you were too modest to tell me."

Peter pulled the sheet of paper out of the third tray, and KC saw that it was a picture of herself that she'd never seen before. She lay on her narrow bed, fully clothed and fast asleep, her dark hair thrown across her face like a veil.

"Hey!" KC said in surprise. "When did you take that?"

Peter grinned, embarrassed. "I'm sorry I never told you," he said. "I came up to see you one afternoon, and your door was open. You looked so peaceful, just like a little kid. I'm glad I had my camera so I could capture the moment."

"Very funny," KC said, moving toward him and slipping her arms around his waist. "But you still haven't answered my question. Why are you printing every photograph you've ever taken?"

"It's not *every* photograph," Peter argued. "Just my more recent stuff."

"Uh huh . . ." KC studied Peter's red-tinted face. His lips were smiling at her, but his eyes lacked their usual warmth. KC felt goosebumps rise on her arms. "Are you *sure* you're not hiding a girl in here?" she asked. "You're being so evasive."

Peter clipped the photo of KC to the clothesline. "I'm sorry," he said. "I'm just distracted. These photographs are for a class assignment. We have to review our work to see how far we've come. You know, where we've been . . . where we're going . . ."

"Hmmm," KC said. "Sounds interesting. I'll bet you'll go further than anyone else in your class. You've got real talent. Even my amateur eye can see it."

"Thanks," Peter said. "But I don't think you're completely objective about me. Someone else might not look at my work the same way."

"I'll admit I don't see *you* objectively," KC said. "I have very definite, very personal feelings about you."

"Oh really?" Peter said, moving closer. "Like what?"

This was it. This was KC's opening to say what she'd come to say. But was it really safe to tell him? KC had the feeling he was holding something back.

But maybe she was just being paranoid again. KC had told herself she was willing to take the risks of being in love. Now was the time to prove it, to say those three little words. KC tried to get her mouth to form the first one. *I.* That shouldn't be so hard. It was just one syllable.

"I . . ." KC said.

"Yes?" Peter said, gazing into her eyes with his steady, hazel ones.

"I . . . don't want to keep you from your work," KC said. "Do what you have to do."

Peter grabbed a magnifying glass and held it over a proof sheet. "So what are these definite, personal feelings?" he asked. "Wait, don't tell me. You've been holding it in for months, but you've finally got to say it. You only want me for my body. Not that I blame you. I work out at least five times a year." Peter sucked in his stomach and tensed his chest, like a bodybuilder.

"That's it," KC said, pretending to snap a picture. "To me, you're just another pretty face."

"It's a sad life," Peter said, shaking his head, "but someone's got to live it."

KC laughed. Peter's sense of humor always made her relax.

"Actually," KC said, "I feel a little more for you than that. But it's been hard for me to focus on my personal life. I mean, I've been so busy with coursework, papers, and tests, not to mention all the social obligations for TriBeta."

"Yeah. I can see how cutting flowers out of construction paper for sorority teas could take up time," Peter teased.

KC grinned. "Well, it does. And now that I've started modeling, it's just one more thing to think about."

"I thought we were talking about me!" Peter joked, taking a yard-long strip of negatives and holding it up to the red light.

"We are," KC said. "Or, we would, if I could just get to the point." She took a deep breath. "What I'm trying to say," KC began again, "is that I'm going to pare down some of this stuff so that I have more time to focus on my studies and my personal life. I don't have any modeling jobs lined up for a while, and I don't have any major projects coming up in my business class."

Peter stuck a tiny red dot next to one of the

negatives on the strip and placed the strip under the lens of a bulky metal machine.

"I know, I know," KC said. "What does this have to do with you? Well, okay, here I go. Out with it. This has been one long, verbal, beating-around-the-bush mostly because I'm too scared just to come right out and say it. But I'm not scared anymore. I'm going to say it. Right now."

Peter turned a knob on his machine and projected an image onto a plain white piece of paper.

KC clutched her elbows, holding them tight against her stomach to shield herself from the explosion that was sure to follow. Screwing up her eyes so she wouldn't have to see Peter's reaction, she tore the words from her throat.

"Peter," KC said, "I love you."

Four

....

"Okay, everybody," Winnie shouted four days later. She jumped up on the beige, leather sofa and waved her hands in the air. "Let's get this video party started. We have to vote on a movie, so I'd like you all to pay attention."

Dash, who lay on a giant pillow spread on the floor of the basement of Forest Hall, didn't mind paying attention to Winnie. He liked her enthusiasm, and her manic grin was contagious. She did make a lot of noise, though. The bells on her boots jingled and the multiple plastic bracelets on her wrist clacked. Winnie was definitely a girl you noticed, but Dash could never imagine dating her. He'd have to wear earplugs.

Who was he kidding? Dash could never imagine dating anyone but Lauren. Right now, she snuggled in the crook of his arm, warm and soft, as the two of them waited for the Friday night video party to start. Lauren's wispy, light brown hair was spread out around her face like a halo, and her pale skin glowed like a translucent pearl. Her eyes were closed behind her wire-rimmed glasses. Tenderly, Dash kissed the tip of her nose. "You sleeping?" he asked.

"No," she said, without opening her eyes.

"Thinking?"

"Sort of."

"About what?"

Lauren sighed and turned her head away from him. A tiny line appeared on her porcelain white forehead. Dash recognized the line. It meant something was wrong.

"What's the matter?" he asked.

"Nothing." Lauren crossed her arms over her patchwork vest, and the line on her forehead grew a little deeper.

Since Lauren wasn't planning to give him any clues, Dash tried to read her face, but it was closed to him. Who ever said girls were supposed to be the open, emotional ones? Lauren always held things in, no matter how strongly she felt. Dash

knew she was afraid to express herself, but
sometimes he wished she'd just tell him if
something was bothering her.

"I am *not* watching that movie," Kimberly
Dayton said to her boyfriend, Derek Weldon.
"It's filled with senseless violence." Kimberly
lounged on a pillow near Dash, her long, lithe,
dancer's body flatteringly revealed in a dark green,
one-piece, stretchy outfit.

"But it's good!" Derek argued as he
simultaneously grabbed a handful of popcorn from
a huge plastic bowl and reached for a slice of pizza
out of the cardboard container. "And the violence
isn't senseless. It's part of the plot!"

"That's my whole point!" Kimberly shouted.

"I'm with you, Kimberly," Faith shouted from
halfway across the room. She sat, alone, on
another big pillow, hugging her knees. "Why
would we want to watch some blood and guts
punchfest when we can see one of the greatest
classics ever made?"

"Yeah! Let's watch something with artistic
merit," chimed in KC, who sat on the floor in
front of the TV, watching Peter help Josh hook up
the VCR. Across the room, Melissa McDormand
sat on the couch with her fiancé, Brooks Baldwin.
Both of them were studying while they waited.

Maybe that was it. Maybe Lauren was upset
because some of the guys wanted to watch a

violent movie; she was very sensitive to violence. She couldn't stand to see any living thing suffer, even in a movie where the blood was obviously fake. She'd cried her eyes out, once, when they were watching a documentary about how tuna fishermen killed innocent dolphins. Dash had never told her, but he'd started carrying extra tissues in the pocket of his denim jacket, just in case she needed them.

"People! People! Please!" Winnie shouted again. "All this arguing isn't getting us anywhere. This is America. Let's vote!"

Josh jumped up beside her, stuck two fingers in his mouth, and emitted a shrill, piercing whistle. Everyone in the room immediately fell silent.

"Thank you," Winnie said, stooping down to pick up two videocassette cases on the couch. "Now, just to go over our choices one more time." She held up the first video, which had a blood-red cover and a darkhaired, ponytailed man kicking another man in the stomach. "This is *Thunderfist*, starring martial artist Jack Harris. It's about an ex-cop who's chased down by drug dealers he's sent to prison. Basically a lot of shooting, bonebreaking, and car chases."

"Yeah!" Derek shouted between bites of pizza. "That's my kind of movie!"

"I've seen it!" Brooks said. "It's great!"

Melissa wrinkled up her freckled face. "I used to

like you," she said, slapping Brooks playfully on the shoulder.

"Or," Winnie announced in a dramatic voice, holding up the other video. "We could see that great 1948 movie classic, winner of no less than eight Academy Awards, *The Fleeting Years*. An epic period romance of the Civil War era, it has everything: hunky leading men, beautiful costumes, forbidden love . . ."

"Hey!" said Josh, who'd jumped off the couch and was back at the VCR. "No fair. You're trying to make this one sound better."

"It *is* better," Winnie said. "How many Academy Awards did *Thunderfist* get?"

"It's girl stuff," Dash said. "Lots of sappy violins playing deep, emotional music while the heroine tries to win her man back." Actually, Dash had seen the movie several times and had practically memorized the dialogue, but he couldn't admit this in public.

"Sexist!" Lauren snapped, poking him in the ribs.

"Ouch!" Dash cried. "That hurt!"

"So let's vote!" Winnie said. "How many for *Thunderfist*?"

Dash raised his hand. So did Brooks, Derek, Peter, and Josh.

"Five votes," Winnie counted. "And how many for *The Fleeting Years*?"

Every girl in the room raised her hand.

"Six votes!" Winnie crowed triumphantly. "We win!" She took a flying leap off the couch and loaded the video into the VCR.

"Talk about sexist!" Dash joked, with a sideways glance at Lauren. "You girls took advantage of your greater numbers to shut us out."

"Men have been oppressing women for centuries," Lauren shot back, her violet eyes flashing behind her wire-rimmed glasses. "We're just trying to even the score."

"Hey!" Dash said, sensing a connection between the line on Lauren's forehead and the hostility in her tone. "I was just kidding. But I have a feeling you're not. Would you please tell me what's wrong?"

Lauren shrugged and turned her head away from him.

"I'm having a little problem with the VCR," Josh called out. "I'll have it up and running in a few minutes."

"Come on, Lauren," Dash insisted, gently removing his arm from beneath Lauren's head so he could sit up and look at her. "If I've done something to upset you, tell me what it is and I'll undo it." He smoothed the hair back from her face so he could see her better.

"Try figuring it out yourself," Lauren whispered, in her breathy, hesitant voice.

"Fine," Dash agreed, trying to think. "I assume it's something that's happened since we got here since you still liked me during dinner. Am I right so far?"

Lauren nodded.

"Okay," Dash continued, "what have I done since we got here? I've eaten three slices of pizza with pepperoni and anchovies. Is that it? Did I eat too much?"

Lauren stuck out her lower lip and glared. "You're not taking me seriously," she said.

"I am!" Dash insisted. "Let me finish reviewing the evening so far. I drank a can of soda, I played a couple rounds of Karate Champ and made it into the top ten, I asked KC three polite questions about her sorority without gagging . . . have I forgotten anything?"

"Exactly," Lauren said, jutting out her lower lip even further.

"Huh?" Dash asked, unconsciously running a fingertip along the stubble on his cheeks. "What do you mean?"

"It's not what you've done," Lauren said. "It's what you *haven't* done. You've forgotten the whole reason you came here in the first place."

"To see a movie . . ." Dash started to say before it all came back to him. "Melissa?" he asked.

"Melissa," Lauren nodded. "I invited you here so you could interview Melissa. You said you needed input from women athletes, but you've ignored Melissa all evening."

"I haven't ignored her," Dash defended himself, though he knew Lauren was right. He really had forgotten. It wasn't that he didn't care about the sex discrimination issue. It just didn't seem that pressing. All he had to do was ask Melissa a couple of questions, maybe find a few other girl jocks to talk to, then dash something off. It wouldn't take more than a couple of hours at the most.

Of course, telling Lauren this would only make her angrier. She'd been working like a slave all week, calling athletes, trying to schedule interviews, reading thick, scholarly volumes on the history of women's rights and taking pages of notes.

The truth was Dash found it difficult to get too excited about the topic. While he was adamantly opposed to discrimination in any form, the notion of female reporters hanging around watching jocks undress and snap towels seemed just plain silly. And since the majority of sports reporters were male, Dash didn't see why all the fuss was necessary.

"I'll interview her right now," Dash said, jumping up. "We have a couple of minutes before the movie starts. You want to come with me?"

Lauren didn't exactly smile, but her lips relaxed their pout.

Dash leaned over to give Lauren his hand and help her up. Stepping around plastic bottles of soda, bowls of chips, and prone bodies on pillows, he made his way across the room. Lauren followed a few steps behind.

"Melissa!" Dash said, flashing a grin at her. "Do you mind if I ask you a few questions?"

Melissa looked up from a fat textbook filled with mathematical symbols and diagrams of molecules. "What kind of questions?" Melissa asked, keeping her finger on her place in the textbook.

"It's for an article I'm working on," Dash explained, taking a pen and notebook out of his pocket. "The subject is important, so I'd like you to think carefully before you say anything." Dash looked over at Lauren, hoping she'd see how seriously he was taking this.

Melissa shrugged. "I'll try. Go ahead."

"Okay," Dash said. "As a female athlete, how do you feel about allowing male reporters to enter your locker room?"

"It's only fair I should warn you," Brooks cut in, before his fiancée could answer, "that you'd better be careful what you ask the future Mrs. Baldwin. She won't pull any punches. She'll tell you exactly what she thinks, even if it isn't what you want to hear."

"I'm ready," Dash said, his pen poised over the open notebook. "Give me your best shot."

Melissa's jaw tensed as she looked at Brooks. "Thanks for the intro, *Mister* Baldwin."

Even though Dash knew Brooks and Melissa were engaged, he still found it odd that someone in college could even think about getting married. On the other hand, Brooks, though a few years younger, seemed more mature and responsible than Dash thought he would ever be. In fact, the more he thought about it, the more perfect Brooks and Melissa seemed for each other—Mr. and Mrs. Serious. Their kids would probably start doing homework before they even started kindergarten.

Melissa turned her freckled face back to Dash. "I don't even need to think about your question, because I know exactly how I feel. I like my privacy, especially when I'm changing my clothes. The last thing I want when I'm stark naked is to be ogled by some male reporter."

This was exactly what Dash had been hoping to hear. An answer that made the issue so clear, even Lauren would have to admit there was nothing to argue about. Then Dash could forget he'd ever heard about this locker room story.

"Let me just rephrase your answer so I understand exactly what you mean," Dash said. "You're saying that you don't want a male reporter in your locker room?"

"Exactly," Melissa confirmed. "And I'm sure

the other female athletes feel the same way. We always answer reporters' questions in a special interview area after we've showered."

Dash turned triumphantly to Lauren. "You see?" he said. "That's all there is to it. It's an easy equation. If the women don't want male reporters invading their privacy, then why should women be allowed to burst in on the men?"

"Because the men don't have interview areas for women reporters," Lauren answered.

"Well, that's because on campus, at least, there have never been any female sports reporters," Dash said.

Lauren opened her mouth to speak, but no sound came out. Her face started to turn red and she clenched her fists.

This wasn't the reaction Dash had been expecting. "What's wrong?" he asked. But Lauren didn't reply. The line on her forehead had multipled to three, and her soft lips were pressed together in a thin line.

"I fixed it!" Josh proclaimed, pressing the play button on the VCR.

"It's starting!" Winnie shouted, turning down the lights and dragging a pillow over in front of the television.

"Let's watch the movie," Lauren said tersely.

At the same time the tape was starting to roll,

Liza was tramping across the dorm green at high speed. She was late for the video party because her scene rehearsal for acting class had run late.

I really have to get some flats, she told herself for the hundredth time as the spikey heels of her gold lamé pumps sank into the damp earth. She wore a matching gold lamé jumpsuit which shimmered in the moonlight, and a brand new sheer chiffon, leopard-spotted scarf which she'd bought especially for the video party. Liza wanted to look especially nice just in case there were any available guys there.

She hadn't forgotten to keep her eyes open for a fabulous guy for Faith, too. He had to be handsome, intelligent, funny, sensitive—in short, perfect—so Faith could see what a good friend Liza had been to find him.

Liza teetered down the steep hill leading to Forest Hall. When she reached the dorm's clear glass door, she pushed it open and found herself standing in the middle of a two-man volleyball game. A regulation volleyball net, suspended up near the ceiling, cut the sterile lobby in half. On either side of the net, a towering, hulking guy swatted at an airborne volleyball with thick, powerful arms. The only problem was, the ceiling was low, so the two players kept bouncing the ball off the ceiling, leaving little dents in the white acoustic tiles.

Though Liza was in a hurry to get to the video party, there was an even greater opportunity here which she couldn't miss. These were guys. Cute guys. Potentially single guys. Guys she could introduce to Faith.

The volleyball player on Liza's side of the net had shaggy, blond hair and smooth, tan skin. The guy on the other side was well over six feet tall, with thick, black hair, olive skin, and a long, thin nose with a slight bump in the middle. He wasn't wearing a shirt, and his broad-shouldered torso looked like an anatomy chart of all the muscles.

Liza's instincts told her she'd struck a potential gold mine.

"Eat this and die!" shouted the dark-haired guy as he spiked the volleyball over the net. The ball slammed into the linoleum floor and bounced all the way up to the ceiling, leaving another indentation.

The blond guy laughed. "You ought to hire yourself out to the Pentagon as a mobile missile launcher, Wide Man. Try that on Tuesday when we play Applegate."

The longer Liza watched, the more she was sure that she'd found the guy for Faith. Even better, she might have found one for herself.

"Excuse me!" Liza said, marching into the center of the lobby and standing underneath the net while the ball sailed overhead. "Pardon me for interrupting—" Liza's words were cut off when the volleyball hit her squarely in the backside. "Oomph!" Liza said, falling forward, her heavy tote bag sliding off her shoulder and hitting the ground with a thud.

"Sorry!" said the darkhaired player. "That was my fault. I guess I lost control of the ball." He grinned at Liza, displaying even, white teeth. His deepset eyes were a swirling, marblized mixture of green and brown.

Liza smiled coyly up at him. "Men always lose control when they see me. Not that I blame them." She stuck one hand on her hip and assumed a sultry expression.

The blond guy laughed. "Hey, that's pretty good!"

"What is?" Liza asked.

"Your impression of Mae West. You sort of look like her, except for the hair."

Liza hadn't been doing an impression of anyone, but that didn't matter. She'd gotten the guys to pay attention to her.

"I'm Liza Ruff," Liza said, shoving her hand into the large paw of the darkhaired guy. "Who are you?"

The guy grinned. "Jason Weidemann," he said. "And this is my buddy Scott Sills."

Scott didn't shake her hand, but Liza didn't care. She was too busy swooning. Jason was definitely interested in her! Why else would he be smiling?

This was going even better than Liza had hoped.

"You know," Liza said, "I couldn't help overhearing you talk about the Applegate game on Tuesday. Are you both on the volleyball team?"

Jason grinned. "Seventeen and zero. Shooting for eighteen straight victories."

"That is so incredibly fascinating," Liza said, though she could care less about volleyball or any other sport. "I saw one of your games last week. I also saw that there were news cameras there. You guys must be celebrities by now."

"I got interviewed on 'Sportswatch'," Scott said with a dimpled grin. "It's going to be aired Sunday night on national television."

"Wow!" Liza said, with real interest. "You know, I was interviewed on the news myself, recently, during *Week at the U*. I'm a performer. Perhaps you happened to catch me in the Follies or at a benefit last weekend . . ."

"Hey, Scott," Jason interrupted, plucking a T-shirt off a chair. "We should get over to The Pub. They're probably waiting for us."

"Who?" Liza asked. "Your girlfriends?"

Scott laughed. "I wish. The people we're meeting are a lot bigger and uglier."

"Yeah!" Jason agreed, pulling the T-shirt over his head.

"That's too bad," Liza sympathized. "Especially when there are women right here on campus, beautiful women, who would love to get to know you better."

"Oh yeah?" Jason asked, his eyebrows rising. "Do you know any?"

"As a matter of fact, I do," Liza said, not mentioning that she was one of them.

"Well, send 'em over!" Scott said. "We'll buy 'em a drink."

"Where shall I send . . . them?" Liza asked.

"We're going to The Pub right now," Jason said. "It's a sports bar right off campus on Center Street."

"Tonight's no good," Liza said thoughtfully, wishing there were some way she could drag Faith out of the video party.

"We're there almost every night," Scott said. "You can usually find us at the pool table."

"Then we'll come tomorrow night," Liza promised. "In fact, I may even have a way for you to get more publicity," she added, suddenly thinking of Lauren. Lauren had said she was having trouble getting interviews with the volleyball players. If Liza brought Lauren along, Lauren would have the perfect opportunity to talk to them. Talk about efficiency. Liza would be strengthening two friendships at once!

"Sounds good," Jason said, slipping a denim jacket on over his T-shirt.

"Just don't forget me when you see me

tomorrow," Liza said. "I expect a *warm* reception."
She looked up at Jason from under half-lidded eyes.

"Just wear that outfit again," Jason said, "and I
won't have any trouble heating up." The sound
of Jason's laughter followed him out the door.

Brooks clasped Melissa's hand firmly as the two
of them walked together under the starless,
overcast night sky. *The Fleeting Years* had run
almost four hours. When it had ended and the
lights had gone on, every girl in the room had
been wiping her eyes, even Melissa.

Brooks had been struck by Melissa's tears. She
seldom cried and had certainly not wept when
they'd both been rescued from the whitewater
rapids where they nearly drowned a few weeks
ago. But that day had turned out to be a cause for
joy, not tears. Melissa, fearing she'd lost Brooks
forever, had realized how much she'd loved him
and had finally agreed to marry him.

"So," Melissa said, her voice showing no trace of
the emotion she'd displayed earlier. "I know it
wasn't *Thunderfist*, but how did you like the
movie?"

Brooks moved closer to her and wrapped an arm
around her slender waist. "Well, it wasn't exactly
my style, but the wedding scene was really nice.
All those flowers . . . Have you given any thought
to what kind of flowers you want at our wedding?"

Melissa shrugged. "Not really. We might not be able to afford flowers, anyway."

Brooks felt a sharp, stabbing pain in his chest. Melissa was trying to be stoic, but he could hear the hurt in her voice and he blamed himself. Every girl wanted a huge, beautiful wedding with lots of guests and presents, a multi-tiered cake, and a long, white dress. There was no way he and Melissa would have a wedding like that, though. Neither one of them had a job to pay for any of the expenses, and since Melissa's father was unemployed and her mother was a housekeeper, they wouldn't be able to offer any help. Melissa was being cheated of a dream, and Brooks felt personally responsible.

"We'll have flowers," Brooks promised. "As many as you want. We'll go on a honeymoon, too, even if I have to borrow the money from my father. Maybe he'll give us the money as a wedding present."

"I'm surprised he's even speaking to you, let alone giving you money," Melissa said. "If my son were a freshman in college and had called to say he was getting married, I probably would have disowned him."

"Those are your own fears talking," Brooks said, playing with her thick, red ponytail. "My dad's never told me what to do or what not to do; he trusts my judgment. And I've never proven him wrong."

"You *do* inspire confidence," Melissa admitted, letting her head rest on Brooks's shoulder.

They walked in silence across the broad lawn, still damp from a recent drizzle. There was no moon, but Brooks could make out the lighter gray of clouds drifting over darker gray sky. The only light came from cast iron lampposts ringing the green with a band of yellow gold.

Brooks wrapped his arm protectively around Melissa's shoulder. "As long as I'm here, you won't have to be afraid of anything," he promised. "I'll be there for you as long as I live."

"Wow . . ." Melissa said softly. "That sounds like a long time."

"That's what marriage means," Brooks said wisely. "It's a lifetime contract. But when you love the person, it's not a burden. Isn't that right, Mrs. Baldwin?"

Melissa's body tensed, and she pulled away from Brooks's embrace. "That's the second time you did that!" she shouted. "I don't like it."

"Don't like what?"

"I don't like being called Mrs. Baldwin! It's not my name."

"Not yet," Brooks said. "But it will be. I'm just trying to get used to saying it."

"Well, don't bother," Melissa said, picking up her pace so that Brooks had to work hard to keep up with her. "No one is going to call me Mrs.

Baldwin."

"Why not?" Brooks asked, his sturdy legs striding vigorously. "That will be your name after we get married."

"Baldwin's not *my* name. It's *your* name," Melissa said, looking back at him over her shoulder. "My name is McDormand. It's the family I come from; it's part of me. Getting married won't change that."

"Of course it will!" Brooks argued. "Women always take their husband's names."

"Not anymore," Melissa countered. "Lots of women keep their maiden names, and I'm planning to be one of them."

"But it would just confuse people. They'd think we were two separate people instead of a married couple."

"We *will* be two separate people," Melissa said. "I wouldn't have it any other way. If being married means I lose my individuality and don't even have a name of my own, then I don't want to get married."

"I think you're blowing this way out of proportion," Brooks said. "Besides, Baldwin's a nice name."

"That's because it's *yours*," Melissa said, stopping so suddenly that Brooks nearly crashed into her. "How would you feel if you had to give it up and be called Mr. McDormand for the rest of your life?" Melissa planted her hands on her hips and waited for an answer. "Well?"

Brooks stared into Melissa's angry face and tried to formulate some sort of response, but he was at a loss for words.

Five

....

"**I** can't believe we're doing this," Faith whispered to Lauren as the two of them followed Liza through the drizzly streets of downtown Springfield on Saturday night. The pavement was slick and shiny with rain that had been falling off and on since yesterday.

Faith, Lauren, and Liza were on their way to The Pub, where Liza had assured them they would each find what they were looking for. She had promised Faith a new boyfriend and Lauren some volleyball players to interview for her article.

Faith's teeth were chattering, and a puddle she'd stepped in several blocks ago had worked its way through the soles of her black cowboy boots so that her toes were cold and damp. Lauren, walking beside her, was also shivering, though she wore her green satin bomber jacket and a black wool scarf.

"I can't believe we let Liza talk us into this," Faith said, pulling the lapels of her denim jacket tight around her like a shawl.

"Me neither," Lauren said, her breath making puffy clouds under the glow of the street lights. "But she can be very convincing."

Faith wanted to believe in Liza. She wanted to believe that going to The Pub tonight would really change her life, but she didn't trust Liza's taste in men.

"I should go back to the dorms," Faith said, loud enough so Liza could hear. "Who am I kidding? I'm not the kind of girl who has a wild Saturday night. I belong in a flannel nightgown, sitting in front of a TV, drinking hot chocolate."

"And why should these volleyball players want to talk to me?" Lauren added. "They wouldn't answer my phone calls or give me five minutes at the gym."

"Trust me," said Liza, with an exaggerated wink. "I had those two guys eating out of the palm of my hand last night. They'll do whatever I tell them to."

Liza tightened the clear, plastic rainbonnet protecting her fluffy, orange curls. She wore a bright orange plastic raincoat over a shiny, black lycra unitard, and the same sheer, leopard-spotted scarf she'd worn the night before. Her gold lamé pumps were covered by black, high-heeled rubbers. Faith had never seen high-heeled rubbers before, but leave it to Liza to find them.

"But how do you know this Scott guy will even like me?" Faith asked. "You said you only spoke to him for a couple of minutes. I'm probably not even his type. And I'm not exactly into jocks myself."

Faith thought back to Brooks, who had been her boyfriend for four years in high school. He had also been a star player on the Jacksonville High School soccer team. Faith had faithfully attended his games, but she'd always brought something she could read on the sly, usually a paperback play which was small, thin, and easily concealed.

Faith and Brooks had broken up right after they'd arrived at U of S, and Faith had dated only casually since then, not counting an intense fling with Christopher Hammond, a senior directing a show Faith had worked on.

Faith's other experience with a jock, Sheldon Copperstein, had also been a complete flop. KC had introduced Faith to Sheldon, a varsity player on the U of S soccer team, but after two extremely short dates, they'd run out of things to talk about.

"No more negative talk!" Liza proclaimed as she

led them down Center Street, beneath the red, green, and white streamers cascading from Luigi's restaurant. "This evening is going to be a dream come true for both of you. Lauren, you'll get so much valuable information for your article that you'll win your debate on Wednesday and maybe even the collegiate version of a Pulitzer prize."

"The collegiate version?" Lauren asked dubiously. "I don't think there is such a thing."

Liza shrugged. "Well, you'll win something. And you, Faith, are about to embark on a night of romance and mystery. Your eyes will meet across a crowded room. It will be love at first sight. Slowly, he'll approach you as your heart beats wildly."

"You should write fiction," Faith suggested.

"Okay, maybe I'm overstating it, but it's still going to be great," Liza said, as she sidestepped a puddle and tottered across the street in her high heels.

On the opposite corner stood a white-shingled building with a glass window and a neon sign that said "The Pub." Other neon signs also hung in the window, advertising different brands of beer. As Faith followed Liza and Lauren across the street, she became aware of a steady throbbing.

"Here it is!" Liza announced as they approached the entrance. The throbbing grew stronger. "We're going to take this place by storm. Those guys won't even know what hit 'em."

Liza flung open the wooden door, and rock music blasted out.

The air inside was thick with smoke. The bar had shiny, colorful banners hanging over it, one for each of the U of S men's sports teams. Tall, muscular guys jammed against the long, wooden bar, drinking out of clear glass mugs with the U of S logo.

Covering nearly the entire far wall, opposite the bar, was a large TV screen on which a basketball game was in progress. Dozens more guys were crowded in front of the screen, cheering, drinking, playing pinball, crushing empty beer cans against their foreheads, or ripping open full beer cans with their teeth and draining them dry without coming up for air.

Faith shot Lauren a helpless look. "I think we're the only women within three blocks of here!" she shouted above the music. How on earth could she ever meet a guy in this place? There was no way a jock was going to find her more interesting than a basketball game or a can of beer.

Lauren, whose wire-rimmed glasses were beginning to fog from the steamy air, nodded grimly. "We don't exactly belong."

Even Liza seemed to have wilted since stepping through the door. She looked around uncertainly, as she took off her bright orange raincoat.

"Maybe this wasn't such a good idea," Faith said, but Liza seemed to have already recovered her confidence.

"There they are!" Liza yelled, barging through the wall of male bodies toward the pool table that stood in the center of The Pub.

Faith tried to follow, but the bodies that had parted for Liza filled in again. "Excuse me!" she shouted, finally managing to worm her way through.

When at last she and Lauren found themselves near the pool table, Faith saw Liza tugging on the sleeve of a tall, dark-haired guy, who was sitting on a bar stool. He seemed oblivious to Liza. His eyes were riveted to the basketball game, alternately cheering and booing as the players on screen raced from one end of the court to the other. Faith wondered how he and the other guys could even follow the action, since the television announcers were drowned out by the music blaring from giant stereo speakers.

"I'm starting to get a headache," Lauren said to Faith, her fingers in her ears. "How am I going to do an interview when I can't even hear myself talk?"

Liza tapped the shoulder of an adorable looking guy with blond hair and a healthy tan. But he was leaning over the pool table, preparing to hit the cue ball with his stick, which was why he ignored

Liza completely.

"This is ridiculous!" Liza shouted, as she joined Faith and Lauren. "It's too loud in here for me to catch their attention."

"We could leave," Faith suggested, but Liza's blue eyes suddenly lit up and her lips spread into a high voltage smile.

"I've got it!" Liza said. "Stay close." She walked toward the dark-haired guy again, and began patting his long thighs as if she were testing a mattress. Suddenly she heaved her fleshy body up onto his lap. That got his attention. "Remember me?" Liza screamed, wiggling her dark brown eyebrows and puckering her lips seductively. "I said I'd come back with my girlfriends. Well, here I am!"

"Here you are," the guy agreed with a wan smile.

"Faith, Lauren, this is Jason Weidemann," Liza introduced them as she snaked her arms around his neck.

"Hi," Faith said, looking down at the pointy tips of her black cowboy boots in embarrassment.

"Lauren's a reporter for the *Weekly Journal*," Liza said. "She wants to do a personal profile on one of you winning players, but of course practically the whole team is beating down her door, trying to be the chosen one. Maybe if you're really nice to her, she'll pick you."

"Is that right?" Jason asked Lauren, shifting on the stool, trying to get comfortable.

"Well, actually," Lauren started to say, but Liza cut her off.

"Here's the deal," Liza told Jason. "If you're really nice to me, I'll put in a good word to Lauren, and maybe you'll be the one she'll feature."

"Hm. . ." Jason said, looking down at Liza's skin-tight outfit. "I guess it wouldn't be so bad."

"Good!" Liza said, hopping off his lap. "Start answering some of her questions, and I'll be back in a little while. You're next, Faith."

Faith shielded her eyes with her hand as Liza pulled her closer to the pool table. "This is so embarrassing!" she started to say, but Liza wasn't listening.

"Scott!" Liza shouted at the tan, blond guy who was now leaning against the table holding his pool stick. "Here's the girl I said I'd introduce to you. This is my roommate, Faith Crowley. Well? What do you think? Isn't she a beauty?"

Faith wanted to crawl under the pool table and hide. She should have known better than to let Liza play matchmaker. Liza was about as subtle as a bulldozer. After an introduction like that, how could Faith even look this guy in the face, let alone go out with him?

"She's a knockout!" Scott said, with a dimpled

smile at Faith.

Almost involuntarily, Faith found herself smiling back. "Hi," she said shyly.

"Well," Liza said, "now that you've met, I'll leave you two lovebirds alone." She went back to the stool where Jason was talking to Lauren.

Liza had actually done it. Liza had given Faith an opportunity to break out of her rut with an adorable guy who actually seemed interested in getting to know her. Now it was up to Faith. But she didn't know what to say to hold his interest. The most exciting thing that had happened to her in the past week was that she'd stubbed her toe in the shower.

"Are your feet wet?" Scott asked, pointing to the floor where Faith's cowboy boots had left footprints.

Faith looked down at her feet. "They're a little bit cold," she admitted. "It's still raining outside."

"Well, you don't want to become sick. You should take off your boots and dry your feet."

Scott's eyes shone with kindness, and Faith started to feel a little more comfortable. "I don't think I'd dare take my boots off in here," she said. "They'd be crushed by someone in five minutes."

"Come with me," Scott said, picking up a bottle of beer resting on the edge of the pool table. "I'll show you my secret hiding place."

Scott led her behind the giant TV screen and

through a battered metal door. On the other side of the door was a quiet room with old couches and chairs. A few couples were scattered along the couches, chatting quietly. At the far end of the room was a working fireplace. A fire crackled evenly from logs that looked a little too perfect to be real.

Scott closed the door, blocking out the loud music, and pulled two chairs in front of the fireplace. "Sit down," he invited. "Take your boots off."

"Is this a real fireplace?" Faith asked, sinking into the deep cushions and pulling off one boot.

"It's a gas flame," Scott said, "but the fire's real. It should warm you up in no time. Here. Why don't you put your feet on my lap?"

"They're cold and clammy," Faith warned.

"My favorite kind."

Faith rested her heels on the denim fabric of Scott's black jeans, and Scott angled his chair so the soles of Faith's feet would be aimed directly at the fire.

Faith giggled, embarrassed. "I feel a little silly," she admitted.

"Why?"

"Well, this just seems sort of . . . intimate for two people who've just met. I mean, you don't even know me, but you already know that I have a hole in my sock."

"I never worry about stuff like that," Scott said. "I've got holes in everything I wear, some of them on purpose."

"On purpose?"

"Definitely. It drives my mother crazy every time I go home for vacation. She tells me I look like a bum. Sometimes, when I get back to school, I discover she's thrown out some of my clothes and replaced them with new ones."

"That's nice of her," Faith said. The warmth of the fire was starting to work its way through her socks, sending soothing heat up through her feet.

"Not really," Scott said. "She's just afraid that if I look like a bum, someday I'll become one."

"That's silly. Why should it matter what you wear?"

Scott shrugged. "It matters to her. And my dad. And my older brother and sister. You should see them. They look like a family of mannequins with stethoscopes around their necks. Dr. Sills, Dr. Sills, Dr. Sills, and Dr. Sills."

"Wait a minute," Faith said. "Do you mean everyone in your family's a doctor?"

"Except me," Scott said cheerfully, holding his hands up to the fire.

"Well, you're still in college," Faith said. "Are you planning to go to medical school?"

Scott frowned. "The only way you could drag me into medical school is if I were a cadaver."

Faith laughed. Scott was turning out to be even nicer than she'd expected. She'd definitely underestimated Liza's taste in men. Maybe she'd underestimated Liza all along.

Of course, the conversation hadn't turned to the subject of Faith yet. That's when everything would start going downhill. She'd start talking about how the colors ran on her favorite T-shirt when she did her laundry last week, and he'd start looking for the nearest emergency exit.

Of course, she could talk about the plays she'd directed at U of S—that was sort of interesting— but it was all in the past. She'd barely lived yet, and she already felt like the best part of her life was behind her.

Faith's feet were almost dry. Maybe now would be a good time to leave, before Scott realized how dull she really was.

"Well, thanks for the fire," Faith said, lifting her feet off Scott's lap. "I really should be getting back to campus." She started pulling on her cowboy boots.

"No way!" Scott protested. "You just got here."

"I'm really not that much fun in a bar," Faith said, figuring he might as well know the truth. "I can't crush a beer can with my bare hands and I don't know how to play pool."

"I'll teach you!" Scott said, jumping out of his armchair. "I'm an expert."

Faith hesitated. The idea of spending more time with Scott was tempting, but it would only make it harder to face Scott's disappointment later.

"Come on," Scott said, grabbing her hand. "I practically *own* the pool table in there. I'll teach you everything you need to know."

Before Faith could protest, he'd pulled her back out the metal door and led her through the noisy crowd toward the pool table.

"I'm sure I won't be any good," Faith warned.

"There's only one cure for that," Scott said, placing an arm across her shoulder. "As Coach Brandes always says—*practice*! Come on. I'll show you what to do."

"But aren't we interrupting?" Faith said, eyeing the jocks ranged around the table.

"These guys'll do anything I say," Scott said with a wink, "mostly because they all owe me money. And I say, let's start over. We'll make it you and me against those two big, ugly dudes over there." Scott nodded across the table at a guy with red hair and freckles, and a black guy with a moustache. "Rack 'em up, Chuck," Scott told the redhead.

While Chuck gathered the colorful balls from the table and put them inside a triangular plastic frame, Scott handed the polished wooden stick to Faith. "Let me see your form," he said.

Self-consciously, Faith leaned over the green felt table and hooked her left index finger around the end of the stick. With her right hand, she gingerly pushed the stick through her curved finger.

"That's not bad," Scott said, leaning over her and placing his left hand over hers, "but I think you'd have more flexibility if you knotted up your finger like this and balanced the cue on top."

Faith tried to follow Scott's instructions, but she was too overwhelmed by the warmth of his body brushing against hers.

She inhaled his musky cologne and sighed. Maybe she'd been too quick to write off all jocks. After all, the only ones she'd known had been soccer players. Maybe volleyball players were different.

"That's better," Scott commented as Faith copied the position of his finger. "I think you're ready for the big time." He stood up. "So, how much are we playing for?"

"Huh?" Faith asked, regretting that his body was no longer close to hers.

"What's the wager?" Scott asked. "It's no fun unless you play for cash. Why do you think these guys owe me so much money? So what do you think? How much should we take them for?"

Faith didn't know how to answer. This wasn't exactly big-time gambling, but she'd never even played the lottery. "You decide," she said weakly.

"Five bucks," Scott declared.

"No way," Chuck protested. "I already owe you ten."

Scott shrugged. "You can add it to your tab. I'm in no hurry to collect."

"Uh, look Scott," Faith said, laying the pool cue across the table, "I really don't think I'm the partner you want for this game. I'll only drag you down."

"I can carry you," Scott said confidently. "Besides, don't worry about how well you play. Just relax and have fun." Scott suddenly looked up at the giant stereo speakers near the ceiling. "It's like the song says," Scott said, singing along with the blaring music, *"Party on and have a good time! Yeah! We're all here to have a good time. Party On!"* Scott started swinging his hips and dancing around the pool table. "Come on!" Scott said, as he came back around to her side. "Dance with me!"

Faith half-heartedly joined him, but she felt stupid, as if everyone in the crowded bar was staring at her. Her arms felt like wooden clubs swinging from her shoulders, and she shifted her weight stiffly from one foot to the other.

"You can do better that that," Scott encouraged her. "Just let the beat carry you along. *Party on! Party on! Have a good time now!"* he sang.

Faith felt like the words in the song had been written specifically for her. It had been months since she'd had any sort of social life, and it was almost like her "fun" muscles had atrophied from lack of use. She'd forgotten how to have a good time. No wonder she felt so dull.

"Party On!" Faith tried to sing along, but her voice sounded desperate and screechy, like someone who was trying too hard to be something she wasn't.

Chuck, who'd lined up the triangle full of balls at one end of the table, stepped between Faith and Scott. "We're ready for you, poolshark," Chuck told Scott. "But there's no way I can face you without a drink. I'm going to go get us some beers. Who wants?"

Scott pulled a twenty-dollar bill out of his back pocket. "Get me a mug of whatever's on draft," he said. "How 'bout you, Faith? What do you want to drink?"

Faith didn't know what to answer. She was pretty sure that when Scott said *drink*, he meant alcoholic drink, but Faith had never drunk anything stronger than ginger ale. Neither of her parents were drinkers, and Faith had never been much interested in trying alcohol either. But maybe that was part of the reason she felt so boring. She was too straightlaced. She didn't drink or smoke, she'd never tried drugs, she didn't even drink coffee!

"I can't drink," she said. "I'm underage."

Scott smiled and put his arm around her. "You and almost everyone else on campus is under twenty-one," he said. "I'm only nineteen and Chuck here is twenty."

"Then how . . ." Faith began to ask, but Scott had already pulled out his wallet and flipped it open.

"Fake ID," he answered, showing her a doctored driver's license. "Everyone has one. It's the only way you can party in this town. And of course, we're just doing our civic duty, keeping the bars open. They'd all close down if they didn't have our loyal patronage."

Faith studied Scott's driver's license, which showed his birthdate to be three years earlier than it should have been. It was a professional job, with no sign of tampering. "I know I'll sound like a dork for saying this," Faith said, "but isn't it illegal to carry a fake ID?"

Scott laughed and patted her on the head, making Faith feel like she was three years old. "Technically, you're correct," he said, "but it's a very tiny law we're breaking. And what other choice is there? Sometimes if you want to have a good time, you have to take a few risks."

A few risks. Maybe that was the root of Faith's whole problem. So far her life had been risk-free. She was known for comforting other people, giving them tea and hot soup, and for being reliable and safe. But the time had come to break out of her cocoon.

"Let me see that ID again," Faith said. Scott handed it to her and she ran her fingers over the smooth, laminated surface.

Scott had said that everybody had fake ID's. This wasn't exactly true. None of Faith's friends had one. But was there any reason why she couldn't be the first?

Six

....

Finally! After weeks of beating her head against the wall, Lauren was about to get her first, full-length interview with a member of the U of S men's volleyball team. *Leave it to Liza*, Lauren thought with gratitude as she led Jason Weidemann to a slightly more quiet table near the front of The Pub. Directly above their heads, an orange neon sign flashed "Miller Light."

"It's very nice of you to talk to me," Lauren told Jason as they sat down. "I know this is your time off and. . ."

Stop sounding so grateful! Liza's voice warned

from inside Lauren's head. *You're acting like he's doing you the favor instead of the other way around. Be assertive. Act like you have the power to make or break his career.*

"But my time is limited, too," Lauren said with a little more energy, "so I'll need your full attention and cooperation." Lauren pulled a well-sharpened pencil and dog-eared notebook out of her bag. "Ordinarily I record my conversations," she said in a professional sounding voice, "but the music's too loud in here, so speak slowly and distinctly."

Jason shrugged and chugged some beer out of a bottle. "You're the boss. What do you want to know?"

Lauren wasn't sure where to begin. "Uh . . . do you believe in equal rights for women?" she asked, her pen poised over her notebook to write his response.

"I don't know," Jason said, running a hand through his thick hair. "I guess so."

Lauren waited for the rest of his answer, but he was already taking another sip of beer.

"Is that it?" she asked.

Jason tilted his chair back and leaned it against the glass window. "Yeah. Do you want me to go into a long speech or something? Is this a political thing?"

"Sort of." This interview wasn't going

anywhere. Lauren could only blame herself for that. Maybe her question hadn't been specific enough.

"Let's talk about sports reporting," Lauren said. "Do you think women reporters are capable of covering sporting events as well as men?"

Jason shrugged. "I don't think there *are* any women sports reporters."

"As a matter of fact there are several. But that's not the point," Lauren said. "Theoretically . . ."

Lauren noticed that Jason's eyes, which had been focused on her, now flitted towards the door. "My next question . . ."she began, trying to get his attention back. But Jason jumped up out of his chair.

"Dash!" he shouted, as Lauren felt a cold draft of air blow in from the direction of the door. It had to be a coincidence. Maybe there was someone else on campus named Dash. Lauren turned in the direction Jason was facing and saw her boyfriend bound toward their table, a huge grin on his face.

What was Dash doing here? He'd said at dinner that he was going to the gym tonight to play a pick-up game of basketball; that was why Lauren had been free to come here. They'd been planning to meet later in the evening, and Lauren had hoped to surprise him with the results of her interview. She wanted him to see how much she'd been able to accomplish on her own.

"Wide Man!" Dash greeted Jason. They clasped hands up in the air in a high five. "What a surprise to see you here, ha ha. Haven't they set up a cot for you in the back room so you can sleep here, too?"

"I'm just blowin' off some steam," Jason said. "Sorry I missed the hoops, tonight. I promised some friends I'd meet them here."

"Lauren?" Dash asked incredulously. "What are you doing here?"

Lauren rose from the table and kissed his stubbly cheeks. "I could ask you the same question."

Dash grabbed Lauren around the waist and kissed her long and hard on the mouth. "I've missed you," he said. "It's been hours since dinner. How have you been?"

"Busy," Lauren said, eager to get back to her interview. "Jason and I . . ."

"Yeah," Dash said, turning to Jason. "That was my next question. What are you doing with my girl?" His tone was only half-joking.

"Hey, easy, man," Jason said, sitting down and pulling an empty chair from another table for Dash. "She's a reporter. She's just asking me a couple of questions."

"Oh, I get it," Dash said, relaxing and sitting down. "Are you doing research for your article?"

Lauren didn't like the tone in his voice. It was

like a parent or a teacher talking to a little kid. That was why Lauren had wanted to talk to Jason alone. Dash, since he was older and more experienced, had a tendency to take over an interview.

But Lauren wanted to show him that he wasn't the expert, and she the apprentice. "Actually," Lauren said, "we were just getting started, so if you don't mind . . ."

"Of course I don't mind," Dash said. "We're in this together. I was coming to look for you anyway. I called your room right before I left the gym."

"Well, after I finish my interview," Lauren said, emphasizing *my* ever so slightly, "we can go somewhere." She turned back to Jason and picked up her pencil again, hoping Dash had gotten her hint. She didn't want him to start asking Jason questions. "Okay, Jason," she said, "getting back to the issue of women reporters, do you see any reason . . ."

"You know, Dash," Jason said, "I was going to call you. A group of us are driving up to Portland next week to watch the Trailblazers play the Lakers. Do you want to come?"

"What day?" Dash asked. "We've got a debate Wednesday," he said, with a wink at Lauren, "and Saturday night we have an awards banquet."

"It's Friday night," Jason said. "I'm calling

tomorrow to get tickets."

"Sounds good," Dash said. "Count me in."

"Back to my question," Lauren said, raising her voice a notch. It had been hard enough trying to interview Jason without Dash. Now that Dash was here, it was practically impossible. "Assuming a woman is as knowledgeable about a sport as a man . . ."

"The ticket's going to cost you about twenty bucks," Jason said to Dash as if he'd forgotten Lauren was even sitting there. "You can pay me Friday."

"Fine!" Lauren said, with growing impatience. "Jason, please. I still have a couple more questions."

"Catch me some other time, Lauren," Jason said as he rose from the table. "It was great seeing you," he said to Dash, "but I don't want to horn in on your quality time with your girlfriend. I'll call you Friday and tell you where to meet us." He gave Dash another too-cool handshake, and wandered off back toward the pool table.

Lauren watched Jason leave, her breath coming in short, quick gasps. She didn't know who to be more angry with—Dash, Jason, or herself.

"Well, that was a funny coincidence," Dash said, inching his chair closer to Lauren's, "although I'm surprised to see you here. This doesn't exactly seem like your type of place. I mean, it's so loud and so . . .*male*."

Lauren stared at Dash. The more she thought about it, the more she realized that it was his fault her interview had been ruined. No matter what Jason said, she was sure she'd probably never get the chance to ask him her questions.

"So," Dash said, "what do you want to do now? It's still early. The film society's showing an old Spencer Tracy movie. Or we could grab some dessert if you're hungry."

"I'm not hungry," Lauren said, spitting out the words.

"Okay," Dash said good-naturedly. "There's a mixer in Rapids Hall tonight. You want to go to that?"

"No!"

How could Dash be so dense? Didn't he understand that he'd completely ruined her evening? If he wanted to be one of the boys, fine, but not on her time.

"Uh oh . . ." Dash said. "Did I do something wrong again? Or did I *forget* to do something?"

"Don't tell me you can't figure it out," Lauren said. Her heart was beating fast, and she could hear herself breathing, even over the music. "It's perfectly obvious."

Dash screwed up his forehead. "I'm trying to figure it out," he said, "but it would be a lot easier if you would just tell me. No, I'm sorry. I should know better than that. That's what girls do, right? Make you guess?"

"Don't lump me with other women!" Lauren shouted. "You're trivializing me, and the problem we're having."

"*What* problem?" Dash asked. "That's all I want to know. Couldn't you please explain it to me?"

Lauren's fingers were gripping the sides of her chair so hard that her knuckles were white. She couldn't believe Dash was unaware of what he'd done. He'd made jokes about her story at the staff meeting last Sunday, he'd systematically undermined her confidence by making her feel her point of view was irrelevant, and now, just as she was finally on the brink of getting some valuable information, he'd interrupted.

So why couldn't she come right out and say it? She had all the words clamoring inside her head, but it was like there was a locked door keeping them all from getting out—a big metal door like the one keeping her out of the men's locker room.

Lauren glanced over at Liza, who was now dancing on the pool table in her bare feet, trailing her chiffon scarf at the upreaching hands of a dozen gorgeous guys. Liza had walked into this place with Lauren just half an hour ago, barely knowing two volleyball players. Now she had the whole place eating out of her hand, just like she'd predicted.

And why? It wasn't that Liza was pretty or incredibly sexy or even that she had the world's best personality. Liza was *confident*. When Liza wanted to do something, she did it, without agonizing over it.

"All right," Lauren said, trying to keep her voice from shaking. "You want to know what you did? I'll tell you." Lauren took a deep breath and looked Dash straight in the eye. "You ruined my interview! You burst in here, you dominated the conversation with Jason so I couldn't even get a word in, and then you practically sent him away with your possessive attitude toward me."

"That's not true," Dash said. "I never said he couldn't talk to you."

"But that's not the worst of it," Lauren said, her voice shaking. Now that the door had opened, the words were pouring out in a flood. "It's your cocky attitude. You haven't taken any of this seriously from the very beginning. I was kind enough to suggest you interview Melissa and all you did was ask her one question, as if the whole issue could be boiled down so easily. Then, when I finally managed to get an interview of my own, with no help from you, I might add, even though it seems you know some of the volleyball players, you barge in here and keep me from asking any questions."

"I didn't barge in," Dash protested. "I just

happened to be passing by."

"The point," Lauren said, pointing a finger at Dash, "is that you still think this story is 'a simple equation.' Well, I won't let you dismiss it so easily. Nothing about this is simple or equal. Women not being allowed in the men's locker room and men not being allowed in the women's locker room are not the same! Most sports writers are men. Men's sports are more popular than women's. It's never been fair to begin with!"

"Don't point your finger at me!" Dash said. "Talk about attitude. You've had a chip on your shoulder from the very beginning. It wouldn't have mattered what I said or did because you were determined to criticize me either way. You were determined to think of me as a male chauvinist pig, simply because I was male!"

"*I'm* not the narrow-minded one. You say you're for equality, but so far you've acted like this is a big joke. You've made me feel like I'm some silly female blabbering on about nothing."

"You said it, not me," Dash said, rising from the table.

"What's that supposed to mean?" Lauren asked, also rising.

"It means this," Dash said, leaning in toward her so that his face was just inches from hers. "It means that we're wasting our time by trying to work on this story together. You don't want to cooperate. You want to fight. Well that's fine with me."

"That's fine with me, too," Lauren said, staring into his flashing brown eyes.

"I also like to *win*," Dash said, "and that's exactly what I'm going to do. I'll see you at the debate. From now on, it's every man—and woman—for himself." Grabbing his knapsack up off the floor, Dash pushed his way through the bodies, toward the door.

"*Her*self!" Lauren screamed after him.

Seven

Pock! Pock! Thump! Peter swatted at the hard, black rubber ball and tried not to wince as it hit his left hand at thirty miles an hour. Maybe the pain was his punishment for what he'd done to KC the week before. Not that she even knew he'd done anything wrong, but *he* knew. The most beautiful girl in the world had told him she loved him, yet he was keeping a secret from her—a huge secret—which was almost as bad as lying.

Pock! Pock! The ball bounced off Peter's hand and hit the side wall of the handball court. Then it popped up all the way to the ceiling, twenty feet above his head and died in the front left corner before Brooks could get there and return it.

"Our point!" Josh yelled. Peter and Josh were playing Brooks at "cutthroat," two against one, Wednesday afternoon in the gym. Josh's long, brown hair was pushed up off his face by a neon green sweatband and his rumpled T-shirt, formerly white, was now a sweat-soaked gray. His long legs poked out of baggy red shorts and ended in a pair of purple, high-top sneakers. In one ear, he wore a blue, marblized earring.

"You know," Peter said, envying Josh's cheerful frame of mind, "I think you've been hanging around Winnie too long. You're starting to dress like her."

Josh shrugged. "As long as I don't start wearing her mini-skirts, I'm not too worried. I like the way she dresses."

"Hey!" Brooks shouted as he returned from the front left corner with the ball. "Are we playing or talking?" His voice echoed off the ceiling, walls and floor of the cube-like room.

"Give us a break, Baldwin," Peter said, wiping his sweaty face with the front of his T-shirt. "You already beat us the first game. It's time for a breather!"

Brooks shrugged and started hitting the ball to himself. Though his face was just as red as Josh's and his blond curls now drooped dark brown with sweat, Brooks showed no sign of letting up. He ran all over the court, batting at the ball like it was his worst enemy. Peter realized he wasn't the only one with a problem.

"Take it easy, Baldwin!" Peter said. "You'll wear yourself out. Not that we'd mind. It might even up the odds a little bit."

Brooks kept batting furiously at the ball, as if he hadn't heard.

"Brooks!" Peter called to him again, stepping in front of the ball to block it with his body. "What's bugging you? This isn't handball. This is war!" Picking up the ball, which had dribbled to the floor, Peter rubbed the sore spot on his leg where the ball had hit.

Brooks's chest heaved as he walked to the back of the court toward a recessed chamber where he'd stowed his plastic water bottle. "You've got that right," he said, opening the plexiglass door to the small box hollowed out of the wall. "Only I think I'm fighting a losing battle."

"What are you talking about?" Josh asked, taking advantage of the break to grab his towel, which was also in the box. "You're beating us singlehandedly."

"That's not the battle I'm talking about," Brooks said, leaning against the wall and sliding down to the floor. "I'm talking about the battle over names."

"Names?" Peter sat down beside Brooks,

grabbed Brooks's water bottle, and squirted a stream of water into his mouth.

Brooks shook his head so that sweat flew off of his curls. "I promised myself I wasn't going to make a big deal out of this, but it's really been eating at me. Tell me what you think about this. Melissa and I are getting married, right?"

"That's what Winnie tells me," Josh said, sitting down on the other side of Brooks.

"So when people get married," Brooks went on, "the wife takes the husband's name. That's just what people do. But when I called Melissa Mrs. Baldwin last Friday, she yelled at me! She said she wasn't going to take my name, and then she started ranting and raving about her individuality and her family and some other stuff, but basically she was acting like I'd done something criminal. I just don't get it. Is it so wrong for a husband to ask a wife to take his name?"

Josh toyed with the leather lanyard tied around his wrist. "It's not wrong," he said, "but it really depends on what the two people want to do. Lots of women keep their maiden names today."

"But *traditionally*," Brooks said, taking the water bottle back from Peter and squirting his face with it, "most women take their husband's name."

"Times change," Peter said. "You don't have to do something just because that's the way it's always been done."

"Yeah," Josh agreed. "And think how the woman must feel. I mean, all your life you have this name and it's part of you, and then, when you're an adult, you suddenly have to start being someone else. I don't think I'd like that very much."

"That was Melissa's argument," Brooks said glumly as rivulets of water dribbled down his face and neck. "But then how do people know you're a couple?"

"Just combine your last names," Josh suggested. "That's what I would do. Josh Gottlieb-Gaffey." He laughed. "It sounds jerky, I know, but it's fair. McDormand-Baldwin doesn't sound so bad, though. If you love someone, you make compromises. That's how you keep things going."

"But how much do you compromise?" Peter mused, almost to himself. "How much do you give up?" He wasn't thinking about Brooks anymore, but about his own situation with KC. He still couldn't believe KC had told him that she loved him. Those three magic words that he'd never even said himself to any girl. Three words he'd certainly never expected to hear from a tough nut like KC. Three words that had changed everything.

As Peter had stared across the red-lit darkroom at KC's beautiful face, he'd felt the same three words welling up inside him. All he'd had to do was breathe, and they would have come rushing out his lips. But Peter had held his breath, afraid to admit the deepest truth he'd ever known, because of his guilty secret.

Two weeks ago, Peter had been feeling anxious that KC was fast outgrowing him as her modeling career took off. Without telling KC, Peter had entered the prestigious Morgan Foundation Photo Competition. The grand prize was a four-page feature in *Photography* magazine and a year of free study in Europe.

Though Peter had been competing with thousands of amateur photographers from all over the world, he'd made the final cut in the portrait category. That was why he'd been so busy printing everything he'd ever done when KC had walked in. He'd been asked to submit three more photographs. Those three pictures could be his tickets to the finest photography studios in Paris, London, or Florence.

If he went. That was the problem. Peter was almost more afraid of winning than losing, because if he won, he'd have the biggest dilemma he'd ever faced. On the one hand, it would mean leaving KC. Beautiful, classy, intelligent, ambitious KC, the fulfillment of every fantasy he'd ever had. Peter knew how many layers of defensiveness and fear KC had had to rip away before she could admit she loved him. He'd be a fool to let go of her now, after all they'd been through.

But on the other hand, he might always regret giving up a Morgan Foundation grant. Studying in Europe could give a major jumpstart to his career as a photographer. He'd meet the key people in his field, be able to learn from them, and be noticed by them. If he had talent, and Peter was pretty sure he did, they'd recognize it. Now that he was so close to winning, Peter didn't think he could pass up the opportunity, even for KC.

"Peter?" Josh asked. "Are you still with us?"

Peter realized that he'd been picking at a hole in his sneaker for several minutes. "I'm sorry," he said. "What were we talking about?"

"You were asking about making compromises," Josh said, rising to his feet. "What's the matter? Don't you like the sound of Angeletti-Dvorsky? I sort of like it. It sounds like the name of a Russian composer."

Brooks, too, hopped to his feet. "I'll tell you one thing we compromised," he said. "Our playing time. We still have fifteen minutes left on the court. Are you guys up for it or not?"

Peter, eager to change the subject, got up and moved forward to the service box. "What's the score? Three-five?"

"My favor," Brooks emphasized, taking his position behind the twenty-foot mark.

Peter bounced the ball once, then slammed it into the front wall. The ball was good, and for the next fifteen minutes Peter was so intent on keeping it in play that he almost forgot about his guilt.

But as Peter left the gym and hopped on his motorcycle, all the uncomfortable thoughts came flooding back. The thing to do, Peter realized as he rode the long way around campus back to Coleridge Hall, was to discuss the matter with KC. He'd explain his dilemma, tell her how torn he was feeling, make her understand how important it was for him to study in Europe.

He'd explain it as a career move. KC would understand that. She was the most career-oriented person he'd ever met. And even though she might be a little disappointed at the prospect of his leaving, she'd quickly put it in perspective.

Peter's motorcycle roared past the political science building and down Greek row, where the fraternity and sorority houses lined the street. Taking the main road around the dorm green, he pulled up into the driveway behind Coleridge Hall. After locking his bike, Peter headed for the back entrance.

Now that he'd made up his mind, Peter couldn't wait to call KC. They were going to Lauren's debate later that afternoon, so Peter would suggest they meet a little earlier than planned.

The sooner they talked it over, the easier it would be to live with his conscience. Peter climbed the half stairway leading up to the first floor, and jogged the last few yards to his room. His keys were still in his hand, but when he touched the doorknob, the door drifted open. Peter's heart started to beat faster. Had someone broken into his room?

Peter smiled with relief when he saw who was standing inside. It was KC, looking as flushed and excited as the last time he'd seen her.

"KC!" Peter cried joyously, as he opened his arms to hug her. "How did you get in here?"

KC crossed her arms in front of her chest, making it impossible for him to draw her near.

"Hey!" Peter said. "Don't I get a hug?""

"You don't want me to drop my arms," KC warned, her voice cold and distant. "I just might use one of them to punch your lights out."

Peter suddenly noticed a few more details about the room that he hadn't seen before. A few wilted flowers lay on the linoleum floor, their stems twisted and broken. KC's eyes were wet, and a tear was trickling slowly down her cheek. Peter touched the teardrop with his finger.

"KC!" he said with growing alarm. "What's the matter? Did I do something wrong?"

"Wrong?" KC echoed, drawing herself up to her full height of five feet eight inches. "Do you consider keeping secrets from your girlfriend wrong? Do you consider leading someone on wrong, when you really don't have serious feelings about them? How about cheating, lies, and deception?"

"What?" Peter asked, feeling the muscles around his heart constrict. He'd never seen KC so angry. "What are you talking about?"

"This!" KC exclaimed, holding up a sheet of beige stationery. Peter didn't have to glance at it for more than a second before he realized it was the letter from the Morgan Foundation, telling him he'd made the last cut in the portrait competition. "When were you going to tell me?" KC demanded. "Or were you just planning to hop on the next plane to Europe and send me a telegram once you got there?"

"How. . ." Peter started to ask, but KC saved him the trouble of finishing his sentence.

"I came here with the foolish romantic notion of giving you flowers," KC said, her voice heavy with hurt and anger. "Your R.A. let me into your room. But then, when I started looking around for a vase or something to put the flowers in, I found this," KC said, rattling the letter viciously with her hand. "I did find somewhere to put the flowers, by the way."

KC pointed to Peter's trash can next to his desk. A bouquet of daisies, buttercups, and black-eyed susans had been dumped among the crumpled papers, the dark green stems sticking up over the top of the can.

"I was going to tell you about the letter," Peter began, but KC interrupted again.

"I can't believe I opened up to you, trusted you, told you my deepest feelings," she said, pacing around the small room. "And I can't believe you let me. How could you, when you knew you were leaving at the end of the semester? How could you make me believe we had any sort of future together?"

"I'm not going anywhere!" Peter protested. "At least, not definitely. I haven't won anything yet, and there's an eighty percent chance I never will. That's why I didn't mention it. Why should I worry you about something that will probably never happen?"

"That's not the point," KC said. "The point is, you *want* to leave. And you never told me, even the other night after I told you I loved you."

"I didn't want to ruin the moment," Peter said. "It was too special."

"Save your smooth lines," KC said. "I've heard enough of them." Grabbing her briefcase off Peter's bed, she pushed past him and stormed out of the room.

Eight

What a waste!" Liza sighed as she leaned against a white porcelain sink in the Forest Hall bathroom. "Do you know how many women would *kill* for naturally blond hair? And you're dying it brown."

"It's only a temporary rinse," Faith said as she sat on Winnie's metal desk chair with her head bent all the way back into another sink, next to Liza. She couldn't see her roommate, because her eyes were smarting and watering from the sharp, bitter smell of the brown dye Winnie was squirting into her hair.

When Faith had made her big decision to get a

fake ID, she hadn't realized it would involve so much discomfort. But it would all be worth it in the end.

"How's it going?" Faith asked Winnie.

"Everything's under control," Winnie assured her. Winnie stood over her, looking professional with her translucent rubber gloves and plastic bottle of brown hair dye. Winnie also wore her tan rain poncho, an unfortunate reminder of the time Winnie had dyed her own hair.

"Are you sure this dye isn't purple?" Faith joked. "I think purple hair looked better on you than it would on me."

"It wasn't purple," Winnie insisted as she squirted with abandon, squishing Faith's hair in the muddy colored water. "It was fuschia. But I assure you, your hair will be a nice, mousy shade of brown."

"That's the only thing about me that's going to be mousy," Faith said, shifting her head a little to ease the strain on her neck. "My life is already changing. I can feel it. For the first time in months, I feel alive again. I think sometimes you don't realize what a slump you're in until you finally get out of it."

"And they say blonds have more fun," Liza said, laughing. Though she was only "assisting" Winnie, which meant watching, she was also dressed for the occasion in a powder pink labcoat with the name "Bonita" stitched above the breast pocket. Liza wore it when she dyed her own hair its unnatural shade of orange.

"I still don't understand how dying Faith's hair is going to help her get a fake ID," Winnie said, putting the squeeze bottle on the edge of the sink and combing the dye through Faith's hair with her fingers. "She's still eighteen-year-old Faith Crowley."

"Not anymore," Liza said. "Before the day is over, she will also be Cheryl White, age twenty-one."

"Maybe you could explain it again," Faith said. "I'm confused, too."

"Okay," Liza said, producing a small square of cardboard from the breast pocket of her labcoat. "This is the non-photo ID of Cheryl White. She's a twenty-one-year-old senior in the drama department who has been very kind to lend this to us. Coincidentally, Cheryl happens to be around the same height and weight as our friend Faith, as indicated on this ID, but Cheryl's brunette, not blond."

"Hence the hair dye," Winnie said, as she squeezed out the excess dye and rinsed Faith's hair in warm water.

Liza nodded. "But now that Faith's hair is brown, she can go into the student union and tell them that she's Cheryl White, using this non-photo ID card as proof of her identity. Then Faith tells them she's lost her university photo ID.

They'll take a photo of Faith and issue her a new ID card in Cheryl's name, only it will have Faith's picture on it. Get it?"

"I think so," Faith said, as Winnie tilted her chair up and wrapped a towel around her neck. "I'll have an alias, just like a criminal!"

Though Faith knew what she was doing was wrong, she felt a perverse thrill. For the first time in her life, she wasn't going to be plain, old dependable Faith. She was going to live dangerously, try things she'd never tried before, and maybe find a little romance along the way.

She and Scott had lingered at The Pub until three in the morning, long after all their friends had gone home. Then Scott had walked her back to Coleridge Hall and kissed her very sweetly, outside the entrance, while the light rain fell unnoticed around them.

He hadn't asked for her phone number, but Faith blamed herself for that. He probably thought she was a stiff, a goody goody, not someone he could have fun with, but Faith was determined to prove him wrong. Faith was going to show up at The Pub with her fake ID and drink and dance and let go, not just for his sake, but for hers.

"Just don't go overboard like I did," Winnie warned, wiping the extra dye off Faith's face with a damp washcloth. "You remember what a maniac

I was when we first got here, last semester? I was totally out of control."

"How could I forget?" Faith asked.

"Tell me!" Liza said eagerly. "I didn't know you then."

"Well, for one thing," Winnie said, "my dorm gave a wild toga party during orientation. I got so drunk I passed out. The next morning, I woke up in Josh's bed. I couldn't remember if I'd slept with him or not. Not to mention the horrible hangover."

"I'm not going to drink *that* much," Faith said. "I want to know what I'm experiencing while I'm experiencing it. That's the whole point."

"Yeah, but you've never had more than a sip of champagne in your whole life," Winnie said, hopping up on the sink next to Faith and swinging her red rubber rain boots which were stained with drips of brown dye. "You probably have a really low tolerance for alcohol. Even one drink could have a strong effect on you."

Liza rolled her goggly blue eyes. "You sound like somebody's mother!" she said, planting her hands on her wide hips. "Faith's a big girl. She'll know when she's had enough. Besides, the last thing Faith needs is for someone to hold her back. She's held back all her life already."

For the first time since she'd known Liza, Faith was beginning to feel that they were on the same wavelength. None of Faith's other friends—KC, Lauren, or even Winnie—had truly understood what Faith was going through. They didn't understand how badly she needed to make a change, to feel like a different person. KC had even gotten angry that Faith was planning to get a fake ID, saying she was disappointed Faith had bowed to peer pressure.

Only Liza had taken Faith seriously when Faith had confessed how awkward and babyish she'd felt around Scott. Only Liza had come up with a constructive solution, suggesting this plan to use Cheryl White's identity. Only Liza was behind her one hundred percent. The more Faith thought about it, the more she realized how much she wanted Liza ad a friend.

"Don't worry, Winnie," Faith said. "Liza will watch over me when I meet Scott at The Pub. She'll let me know when I've had enough to drink."

"Actually," Liza said with an embarrassed shrug, "I'm not too experienced myself when it comes to alcohol. In fact, I never touch the stuff."

"Really?" Faith asked, genuinely surprised. "You seem so—I don't know—worldly."

"Do you really think so?" Liza asked, pouting at her reflection in the mirror and fluffing her orange hair. While Faith knew Liza was trying to look seductive, the effect was more comic than anything else. Then Liza's reflection looked at Faith. "It's true," she admitted. "I *have* lived. And I certainly know my way around men, but I figure that most people drink to loosen up. I'm already so uninhibited that I'd be afraid to see what would happen if I took a drink. I'd probably start flying around the room, emitting sparks. But that's just my personal decision. I think what you're doing is right for you."

"Within reason," Winnie cautioned.

Liza shrugged. "What Faith wants is passion, excitement. You don't get that by doing things half-heartedly. So I say jump in with both feet!"

"I don't know. . ." Winnie said doubtfully.

Faith looked at Winnie, up on the sink, in her bright red rubber boots and flamingo earrings. It was hard to believe that Winnie, of all people, was counseling caution. Winnie used to be the kookiest, craziest daredevil she'd ever met. Winnie had tried everything at least once. She'd climbed up the side of KC's house in the middle of the night. She'd walked along the ledge of a roof in high school. She'd dyed her hair purple. And she'd had many boyfriends. Faith could count all of hers on less than one hand.

Just because Winnie had calmed down was no reason Faith had to. In fact, Faith was seeing Winnie's past in a new light. Sure, she'd gotten into trouble, but at least she had *done* something, *felt* something. At least the blood was flowing through her veins.

Faith looked over at Liza, who was now sitting on the windowsill, painting over her chipped red nail polish with a new coat of bright orange while singing to herself in a loud, off-key voice. The pink labcoat over her generous figure made her look like a middle-aged beautician. But none of it mattered. People thought Liza was glamorous and exciting because that was the way she thought about herself. And if Liza could do it, Faith could too.

"Voil`a"!" Winnie said an hour later after she'd combed and dried Faith's hair.

Faith studied her new image in the mirror above the sink. It was weird, but even though she'd only changed one small part of herself, she really did look like a completely different person. The dark hair made her look older, more mysterious somehow.

"Well?" Winnie asked. "What do you think?"

"I like it!" Faith said, smiling at her reflection.

"It's you!" Liza proclaimed triumphantly, crowding with Winnie behind Faith so they could see her face in the mirror.

"It's *not* me," Faith corrected her, "and that's what I like about it."

"Do you want me to french braid it for you?" Winnie asked.

"No way," Faith said, fluffing her hair about her shoulders. "I'm not going to do anything the way I used to." She turned to face her friends. "Thanks, you guys. I guess I'm ready for stage two. Do you have Cheryl's ID, Liza?"

Liza produced the card from her pocket. "Do you want me to go with you?"

Faith shook her head. "I'll be fine by myself. You know, it's funny, but even though I've never done anything like this before, I don't feel scared. I feel exhilarated." She took the ID card and put it in the front pocket of her blue jeans. "I'd better get going. Lauren and Dash's debate starts in an hour, and I want to have enough time to get the card and then save a bunch of seats for everybody since I'll be at the student union anyway."

"Save one for me," Liza said.

"Me, too," Winnie said, gathering up her bottles, towels, and comb. "Just be careful, Faith, okay? I don't want you to get into trouble."

Faith laughed. "Do you realize how many times I've said the exact same thing to you?"

"And you were right," Winnie said. "I should have listened to you."

"Goodbye!" Faith said abruptly, not wanting to hear any more. "I'll see you later."

Grabbing her suede jacket off a hook on the back of the bathroom door, she raced down the hall, dodging a hockey puck that came whizzing past her feet. Two huge guys in kneepads and rollerblades came skating after the puck with a hockey stick. Faith laughed as she ran down the stairs to the first floor. For once, she wasn't intimidated by this rough play. She understood it. It was what people did who weren't afraid to take chances. People like her.

Faith practically skipped out the door of Forest Hall. The air was steamy as the hot sun evaporated the moisture from nearly a week of rain. Faith inhaled deeply the fresh scent of warm grass and enjoyed the way her feet bounced against the springy earth.

Then all her good feelings vanished instantly.

Scott Sills was walking straight toward her, not more than a few feet away, looking incredible in ripped, faded jeans and a cut off T-shirt that revealed the four well-defined quadrants of his abdominal muscles.

But that wasn't why Faith suddenly felt bad. She felt bad because he'd walked right past her, as if he didn't even recognize her.

Faith couldn't believe that she'd gone to all this trouble for a guy who didn't even notice she was alive. Yes, after weeks of numbness, she was finally feeling something—agony.

"Faith?" The hand on Faith's shoulder was warm and strong. "Is that you?"

Faith turned around and found herself face to

face with a perplexed-looking Scott Sills. "Hi," she said.

"I almost didn't recognize you. What happened to your hair?" Scott asked. "Are you traveling incognito?"

"Well, actually, it's a long story," Faith answered, greatly relieved.

"I have time," Scott said. Then he looked at his watch. "Uh, actually I'm already late for my sociology lecture."

"It's okay," Faith said. "I understand. I'm on my way to the student union, anyway."

"I'll walk with you."

"What about your lecture?"

Scott shrugged. "It's too beautiful a day to sit in some stuffy classroom. Besides, I'm not learning anything in there. As far as I'm concerned, sociology is the science of what you already know. You learn such obvious things like—people need to be with other people, and people smile when they're happy. You don't even need to read the textbook."

"But aren't you worried about your grades?" Faith asked as they headed across the rolling green. The moment she'd said that, Faith wanted to clamp her lips together. She was supposed to be acting loose and carefree, yet here she was reverting to being a grade-obsessed party pooper.

Scott suddenly leapt gracefully into the air to

catch a purple Frisbee that hovered just above their heads. Then he tossed it to a barking, white dog that wore a red bandanna around its neck. The dog broke into a gallop across the green, catching the Frisbee with its teeth.

"That's Max," Scott said. "At least that's what everyone calls him. No one knows who he belongs to." He took hold of Faith's hand. "But in answer to your question, no, I'm not really worried about my grades. I'm not planning to go to graduate school, and I'm not here to impress anyone with my intellect."

"But don't you worry about what you're going to do when you get out of school?" Faith asked.

It had happened again! Who was this gremlin inside her that made her ask all these serious questions? It was the old Faith Crowley. The blond Faith Crowley. And it was holding the new, mysterious, fun-loving brunette Faith Crowley hostage.

"I'm sorry I asked that," Faith said. "It's none of my business."

"Sure it is!" Scott said. "We're friends, aren't we?" He smiled at her so warmly that Faith felt a little less embarrassed. "To tell the truth, I haven't thought too hard about what happens after I graduate. I'm only a sophomore. I haven't even figured out what I want to major in."

"Definitely not pre-med," Faith said, remembering their conversation by the fireplace.

"*Definitely* not," Scott emphasized. "I'm not going to let my parents brainwash me the way they brainwashed my brother and sister. The four of them work twenty-four hours a day, seven days a week. That's all they ever do."

"It doesn't sound like too much fun."

"You've got that right. My brother's got two kids he never sees 'cause he's always holed up in his office, and my sister's divorced."

"That's not living," Faith said with feeling.

"Yeah. You've gotta live one day at a time and enjoy yourself as much as you can," Scott said, echoing Faith's feelings. "That's what *I'm* learning here. I only got into U of S because I'm a good volleyball player. They didn't want me for my brains. But, hey, I'm not complaining."

Faith felt giddy and light, as if someone had injected bubbles into her bloodstream. Here she was having a heart-to-heart conversation with a guy, and discovering a new approach to life at the same time. She thought back to all the years she'd worked so hard to get somewhere; she'd completely ignored where she was at the time.

Scott stopped walking and planted his hands against the ground. He lifted his legs above his head until he was standing in a perfectly balanced handstand. Then he began to walk on his hands, his arms bulging impressively.

"Wow!" Faith cried. "Are you on the gymnastics team, too?"

"Nope," Scott said, gracefully executing a backflip and landing on his feet. "It's just one of my tricks. I'm sort of like a trained seal."

"What else can you do?" Faith asked.

"You'll see," Scott said, with a wink.

"I hope so," Faith said, "if that means I'll see you again."

Faith almost gasped at her own audacity. She'd never said anything that nervy to a guy in her life. On the other hand, she'd never met anyone quite like Scott before, and she still didn't know what to make of him. He wasn't a rock-steady, well-rounded, straight-A student like Brooks, and he wasn't a slick, ambitious striver like Christopher Hammond.

If anything, Scott was a bit of a lightweight compared to them. But he was charming and carefree, not to mention sexy, which meant he was exactly what Faith needed in her life right now. If only he felt the same way about her.

"You know," Faith said casually, "you're not the only person around here who likes to party. In fact, you'll never guess *why* I'm heading to the student union at this very moment."

Scott's pale, blond eyebrows rose with interest. "I love guessing games," he said. "Let me see—you're on your way to a party?"

"Nope."

"I guess that was too obvious. Okay, let me try again. You're going to buy one of those rancid tuna fish sandwiches they sell there and burn it in protest?"

"Nope."

"You're going for the world record at Ms. Pacman in the video room?"

Faith smiled coyly up at him. "Three strikes, you're out. The real reason I'm going is to get a fake ID card so I can help keep The Pub in business. Just doing my civic duty, right?"

Faith told Scott of Liza's plan. And now that he knew, there was no turning back. She had to go through with it.

"Ingenious!" Scott complimented her. "That's much more creative than what I did. I just changed the date on my driver's license, then had it laminated so none of the bartenders could get too close a look."

They were approaching the student union, a two-story red brick building reminiscent of the unimaginative 1950s style dorms.

"This is where I get off," Scott said as they reached the building. "My sociology class is probably half over by now, but I'm going to at least put in an appearance."

Faith hesitated on the two concrete steps leading up to the glass double doors. She wanted to ask

Scott if she would see him again, but she didn't want to sound too pushy. She'd already hinted at this before, and he hadn't responded.

"Have a nice class," she said, trying to hide her disappointment.

"Thanks," Scott said, turning away. Then he turned back. "Oh," he said, "by the way, are you going to The Pub again this Saturday night? It won't be quiet like last weekend since it'll be right after our volleyball game. And if we win, it will *really* get wild."

Faith couldn't imagine how much wilder it could get, but now was not the time to be afraid. What was it Liza had said? *Jump in with both feet!*

"I'll be there," Faith promised, "with my new ID card."

"Great!" Scott said. "See you there!" He kissed Faith quickly on the lips, then broke into a sprint across the green.

Faith's lips tingled and she felt slightly dizzy. But she wasn't sure whether it was from excitement or fear, because now it was time to put her words into action. The registration office was going to close in half an hour. If she was going to go through with this, she'd have to act now.

So why was she still standing here? What was holding her back?

Common sense? the old, blond gremlin-Faith suggested. *Getting a fake ID probably isn't a very smart idea. You'll be breaking school rules, not to mention the law.*

It was time to silence the old Faith. It was time to let the new, brown-haired, fun-loving Faith out of her cocoon, once and for all.

Though Faith's feet felt glued to the pavement, she forced herself up the two steps and pushed open the glass doors with both hands.

Nine

....

Dash's loafer tapped nervously against the floor of the student union common room as students were filling in the empty rows of folding chairs, murmuring excitedly about the big debate that was about to take place.

"Looks like a good crowd," Greg said to Dash, taking an empty seat beside him, in the front row.

Dash turned around to look. The large room, usually set up with round tables and chairs, had been converted to a makeshift auditorium. The tables were now stacked on top of each other in the back, and the chairs had been lined up in neat rows, broken up every so often by concrete pillars. Facing the audience were two battered, wooden podiums equipped with microphones. All the seats, several hundred of them, were filled, and people were still coming in, lining the back wall and sides of the room.

"Gee, Greg," Dash said sarcastically, "I wonder why there are so many people. Could it have something to do with that huge ad you placed in the *Journal* on Monday?"

Greg looked up at the buzzing fluorescent lights, an innocent expression on his face. "I was just trying to help out my friend Thornton," he said. "You know. Promote freedom of expression and the intellectual exchange of views."

"You were trying to push next week's issue of the *Journal*," Dash said, unconvinced. "I read the ad. '*The Battle of the Sexes!* Featuring Dash Ramirez and Lauren Turnbell-Smythe, award-winning reporters for *The Weekly Journal*. Read their follow-up articles in next Monday's paper.'"

Greg shrugged. "So everybody benefits. Especially you. I know how you love to play a big crowd."

Dash knew that was true, but today he wished everyone in the room would disappear. Everyone except Lauren. Then maybe they could talk calmly about the fight they'd had last Saturday night at The Pub. They'd laugh at how foolish they'd been, take back the words they hadn't really meant.

Dash glanced over to his left and saw Lauren sitting at the other end of the front row, between Liza and Faith. Or, at least, it looked like Faith, but she had brown hair.

Lauren's own hair was pulled back with a navy blue headband and she wasn't wearing her glasses. Dressed in a navy blazer, with gold buttons, over a white oxford blouse and tan slacks, Lauren looked very much as she used to, before she worked for the *Journal* and rebelled against her mother. But it wasn't just the clothes which, Dash was sure, she wore to look "gender neutral." It was the way she twisted her fingers nervously in her lap and kept glancing over her shoulder to see how many people were coming in.

Dash couldn't help feeling sorry for her. He knew how much she hated to speak in front of a large group of people—and for her, a large group meant two or more. She probably hadn't slept well last night, and she probably hadn't eaten much today. Of course, Dash was just guessing since he hadn't even spoken to her since their fight.

The worst part was that it was all so unnecessary. Dash thought the whole sex discrimination issue didn't warrant a debate. But it hadn't been his idea to begin with. Yet, Lauren somehow blamed him for all the injustices ever suffered by women at the hands of men.

That was the trouble with women—they couldn't separate their emotions from their work. If Lauren hadn't gotten so overwrought about nothing, they could be sitting next to each other right now, laughing and figuring out where they were going to eat dinner afterward. If she hadn't insulted him, Dash would have gladly read over her arguments and given her some pointers. He would have toned down his own arguments so as not to take advantage of the fact that she was a shy freshman.

But since they weren't even speaking to each other, Dash had figured out another way to make this issue disappear once and for all. It was a way to make Lauren see that she didn't have to take this so seriously. And, just incidentally, a way for him to win the debate hands down.

The squawk of microphone feedback pulled Dash's attention to the podium on the left side of the audience. A lanky young man with a beard and moustache fiddled with the microphone, tapping against it with his finger. "Can everyone hear me?" he asked, his voice emanating from two speakers in the ceiling.

"Yes!" shouted several members of the audience.

"Good," the young man said. "We've been having some trouble with this microphone. Okay,

everybody. Let's get started. I'm Thornton
Lewis, and welcome to this month's Free Speech
Forum. This afternoon's topic is one that's sure
to get everybody's blood boiling—sex discrimination in sports reporting. Here to debate the
issue are Lauren Turnbell-Smythe and Dash
Ramirez."

Several hundred pairs of hands broke into
applause. Dash hopped to his feet and walked
behind his podium. A few yards away, Lauren,
clutching a handful of index cards, hesitantly took
Thornton's place.

"Go, Lauren!" shouted Liza, pumping her fist in
the air.

Dash leaned against the scratched wood surface
of his podium, and waited for Lauren to begin.

"Good evening," she said, in a soft, refined voice
that was barely audible. "As most of you know,
women have been discriminated against for
centuries . . ."

"Louder!" someone in the audience shouted.

"Oh. Sorry," Lauren said, her face turning pink.
She cleared her throat and started again. "While
women have gained many rights in the past
century, they still don't enjoy the same rights and
freedoms as men . . ."

Lauren read the words right off her index cards,
not once looking up at the audience. Her voice,
not much louder than before, was monotone, and

she spoke too fast.

Why had they ever gotten into this stupid fight? Then Dash could have coached her, shown her that everything she was doing was wrong. You were supposed to make eye contact, sound conversational, make your points clearly. Dash wished there was some way he could help her.

". . . *male chauvinist pigs*," Lauren finished a thought, giving Dash a nasty look. "And you know who you are."

Now that was uncalled for. And unfair. She had no right to make personal attacks. Dash felt some of his anger and resentment return.

Lauren's voice faded to a whisper again, even with the aid of the microphone. "Female reporters are just as capable of covering a men's sporting event as males. And they should be allowed equal access to the players post-game . . ."

"Speak up, Lauren!" Liza chided her from the front row.

"I'm trying!" Lauren hissed.

Dash saw a girl in the audience yawn, and the guy next to her close his eyes. Behind them, two girls had started talking.

While Dash still felt sorry for Lauren, a tiny part of him was glad. She was getting what she deserved for insulting him.

". . . proving that most male reporters are just full of hot air." Lauren was practically shouting now, but the microphone was giving her no help at all. Her voice didn't carry further than the first two rows.

"Can't hear you!" shouted several voices from the back of the room.

Lauren tapped her microphone, but there was no response. "Oh no!" Lauren whispered to Liza and Faith. "This is a nightmare. My microphone's dead! What should I do?" Her violet eyes looked around helplessly until they came to rest on Dash.

Dash knew exactly what she was thinking. She wanted him to help her. To come to her rescue, like a knight in shining armor. And Dash, instinctively, had already taken a step toward her, his mind already working on the problem.

Then Dash gripped his podium, to stop himself from going any further. It wasn't just that he was still angry with her. He wanted to teach her a lesson. Here she was, standing in front of all these people, arguing for women's rights, yet as soon as there was a technical breakdown, where did she turn? To the nearest man. That was the height of hypocrisy, and Dash couldn't let her get away with it.

Ignoring Lauren's pleading eyes, Dash forced himself to whistle a happy tune.

"I don't know what to do!" Lauren cried, ducking behind the podium to see where the microphone's electrical cord went.

"Let me try," Faith said, jumping up out of her seat and joining Lauren at the podium. She turned the microphone upside down and played with one of the wires, screwing it in tighter with her thumbnail. "Testing," she said, her voice screeching so loudly over the speakers that everyone covered their ears.

"Thanks," Lauren said, as Faith sat down. "Uh . . . where was I?" Lauren shuffled through her index cards and dropped one of them on the floor. She'd lost the audience completely by now. "Sorry," she said, growing increasingly agitated. "Okay, as I was saying, women have just as much right to gather information as men. A reporter is a reporter. And as long as men are allowed into the locker room to cover a sporting event, women should be, too. Thank you."

There was a smattering of applause, mostly from Lauren's friends in the first row. Now it was Dash's turn.

Even before Lauren had messed up her speech so badly, Dash had felt guilty for what he was about to do. Now he felt absolutely awful. But it was necessary. This whole thing had gone on too long already. Dash was about to put Lauren—and himself—out of their misery. She might not understand at first, but she'd thank him in the long run.

"A reporter's a reporter," Dash said, pushing aside

his microphone and projecting his deep voice all the way to the back wall of the large room. "Stirring words. Sex-blind words. Words to inspire us all." He grinned and sauntered away from the podium, taking center stage.

"My worthy opponent makes the point that a female reporter should be allowed to enter, at will, a male locker room, stressing her right to gather information. Now, that's very interesting."

Dash strolled a few feet down the center aisle between the chairs and smiled at the people who caught his eye. "Because I've read the Constitution *and* the Bill of Rights, and nowhere, *nowhere*, did I find a clause guaranteeing any citizen, male or female, this right."

Dash stuffed his hands in his pockets, and took a few more steps down the aisle. "Do we have any American studies majors in the audience? Am I right or wrong?"

"You're right!" shouted a guy from the back of the room.

Dash nodded. "But in reviewing that great instrument of political freedom, I did come upon another, very basic right guaranteed to everyone, regardless of race, religion, gender, creed or political affiliation. The right to *privacy*."

Dash returned to the podium. Now that he'd warmed up the audience, it was time to move in for the kill.

"In other words, when male athletes are taking off their clothes, they have the right to do so without the prying eyes of female reporters. My opponent's argument might be valid if we lived in a world where there was only one gender, or maybe if we all were blind. But the fact remains that men and women have certain *anatomical differences* which they might not be eager to display to members of the opposite sex." Dash looked over at Lauren, who was staring intently at her index cards.

"But maybe I'm wrong," Dash said. Lauren looked up in surprise. "Maybe these differences are really insignificant after all. If a reporter's a reporter, it shouldn't matter whether the interviewee is dressed or not." Dash loosened his bright red-and-orange tie and slipped it out of his button-down collar. Then he began to unbutton his shirt.

Lauren watched him, not understanding.

Dash undid the last button. Then, in a single, fluid motion, he pulled off his shirt, revealing his well-toned torso. Lauren, and half the audience, gasped.

"Are we really the same?" Dash asked, directing his question to Lauren. The audience started murmuring and snickering. "If we are, then interview me without being embarrassed. Or take off your clothes and I'll interview you! I'm a reporter, too, you know."

As Lauren stared, dumbstruck, Dash kicked off his loafers.

"What's the matter?" Dash teased her. "You're saying that men don't have the right to privacy, so this shouldn't bother you." He reached for his belt and started to unbuckle it.

"Take it all off!" a girl in the audience shouted.

Lauren's mouth was hanging open, and a pink flush was creeping slowly up her neck.

"Come on," Dash said, walking toward her and grabbing her hands. "Let's strip together, and show the world we're exactly alike."

The murmuring had faded to absolute silence as everyone waited to see what would happen next.

Lauren's face was completely red now, and her eyes were glassy with tears. She was panting, almost as if she were out of breath, and her hands felt ice cold in his.

"Well?" Dash asked. "What do you say?"

A wrenching, choking sob, the loudest sound Lauren had made all day, burst from her throat, and tears spilled from her eyes. Tearing her hands out of Dash's, she ran out of the room.

"I rest my case!" Dash said as the audience burst into laughter and applause. Stepping back into his loafers, he bowed to the audience.

He'd won the debate, but that was the last thing on his mind. All he really wanted, right now, was to find Lauren and explain what he'd done. Grabbing his shirt, he headed out the door after Lauren. He didn't see her in the hallway, but he could hear someone sobbing nearby.

Following the sound, Dash crossed the hall into the dimly lit video game room. He found her hiding behind a "Teenage Mutant Ninja Turtles" game, crying and mopping at her eyes with a damp, crumpled tissue.

"Hi," he said softly. "You okay?"

Lauren turned her swollen, red-rimmed eyes toward him. "Okay?" she shrieked. "After what you did to me in there? I can't believe you even have the nerve to face me. That wasn't debating. That was a cheap stunt done at my expense."

"It had nothing to do with you," Dash said. "I was just having some fun. It was my way of saying that everyone takes this issue much too seriously. You don't have to take it so personally."

"What other way can I take it?" Lauren demanded, trying to blow her nose in the tissue which by now had shrunken to a tiny wad. Dash wished he'd remembered to bring the extra tissues he usually carried for her. "You not only made *me* look like a fool, you made a mockery of all women!"

"Oh, please," Dash said, beginning to lose patience. He'd come here to make up, and all she did was keep insulting him. "Don't get so melodramatic."

"It was a dirty trick," Lauren insisted, giving up on the tissue and using the sleeve of her blouse to wipe her runny nose, "and it wasn't fair."

"Fair!" Dash exploded. "You want to talk about fighting dirty? I'll tell you what's not fair. It's you, demanding equality, but still thinking you can manipulate me by crying like a helpless female. Or thinking I'm going to jump in and help you when the microphone breaks down. Well, I have a major newsflash for you. You can't have it both ways."

"I have never been so insulted in my life," Lauren declared, sniffling loudly. "I'm crying because I'm furious with you, not because I'm helpless."

"You could have fooled me."

Lauren abruptly stopped crying and drew in a shuddering breath. "I'll show you who's helpless," she declared, her voice hoarse. "You want to fight dirty? Fine. But you'd better get out your heavy artillery, because *this is war.*"

Ten

Friday afternoon, Faith lounged with Liza, Lauren, and Melissa on the flat, wooden raft that floated in the middle of Mill Pond. The water surrounding them was choppy from the oars of passing canoes, and the raft bobbed gently up and down. It was the perfect recipe for rest and relaxation, but Faith's body was tense, and her mind was hyper-alert.

What is your name?
Cheryl Ann White.
Age?
Twenty-one.

Date of birth?

October 11, 1970. October 11, 1970. October 11, 1970.

Faith went over and over the details in her head, making sure she had all her lines down pat. Tomorrow night was her big debut as Cheryl White—twenty-one-year-old party girl, drinker, and all-around fun person. Her brand new fake ID was now hidden in her dresser drawer, and tomorrow afternoon she was going to borrow some funky clothes from Winnie to wear to The Pub.

Now all she had to do was keep up her nerve, and she'd be home free.

"You really should have put on some sunscreen," Liza scolded Faith. "I'm wearing number 48, completely waterproof for twenty-four hours." Liza sat upright on the gray, wooden slats of the large raft. Only a few wisps of her orange hair had managed to escape from her pastel pink bathing cap with its white and yellow rubber daisies. Her generous body bulged out of a halter-top white bathing suit that was even paler than her dead-white skin.

Faith laughed. "I don't care if I burn. I'm still young. I'll have plenty of time to play it safe when I'm older."

Faith listened to herself say these words and was impressed at how convincing she sounded. It was almost like playing a part in a play—the part of a girl who was brave and daring and didn't care what other people thought. And maybe, if she played the part long enough, she'd start to believe that was who she really was.

"Suit yourself," Liza said, disgruntled, "but meet me for lunch in fifty years and see who has younger-looking skin."

"I think we'll all look pretty wrinkled by then," Lauren said with a sigh. "Not that I look so great right now." Lauren lay beside Faith. Her eyes were red-rimmed from two days of crying after her disastrous debate with Dash. Her wispy hair was pulled back in a messy ponytail. She'd tried to hide her slightly pudgy body beneath an oversize T-shirt which she wore over her swimsuit.

"You look fine," Faith said ,trying to comfort her former roommate.

"Don't let Dash get you down," counseled Melissa, who drowsed on her stomach next to Lauren. Her coppery, red hair glinted in the strong light, and her racer-back tank suit showed off her impressive back muscles. "He's just a guy. I don't know why we let them get to us this way. Sometimes, I think we're better off without them."

"That's easy for you to say," Liza said. "You've already snagged one."

"I've snagged his ego, that's for sure," Melissa

said, propping herself up on her elbows. "He still thinks that I should give up my whole identity, just because he proposed."

"Is Brooks still pestering you about changing your name?" Faith asked.

"Not exactly. In fact, he hasn't said a word about it since I blew up at him. But I can tell he's really upset about it."

"Men!" Lauren sniffed. "Who do they think they are?"

"Beats me," Melissa said, "but at least I know who *I* am. I'm a McDormand. Not that I'm especially proud of my family—you all know about my father's drinking problem, and we certainly don't have any money or go back to the Mayflower or anything like that. But ever since I was a little girl, I've wanted to be a doctor. Dr. McDormand. Not Dr. Baldwin, or Dr. Anybody Else."

"I know exactly what you mean," Liza said, tucking a strand of orange hair under her bathing cap. "I've always envisioned my name up on a marquee someday, or maybe on a movie poster. Liza Ruff. Nice and short and easy to remember."

"I've already got two last names," Lauren said, "which is more than enough for me. Besides, what if you *do* take your husband's name, and then you get divorced? Do you change it back? Or keep the name of someone you wish you'd never met?"

"I can't plan that far ahead," Faith said, still playing her party-girl role. "I'm going to play it by ear. Whatever sounds best." If only Scott could see her now, Faith thought. He'd say she was a girl after his own heart.

"But there's a principle involved," Melissa insisted. "Why should guys automatically assume we *want* their names? You know, the more I think about it, the angrier I get. Brooks was so—matter of fact about it, like there wasn't even a question to be discussed."

"Very presumptuous," Liza agreed. "Who does he think he is?"

"Well, he may be Mr. Baldwin," Melissa answered, "but I'll never be Mrs. Baldwin, even if we're married for the rest of our lives and have a hundred grandchildren. And if Brooks doesn't like it, I'll just call off the engagement."

"That's telling him!" Liza cheered. "Show him who's boss!"

"I wish I could do that to Dash," Lauren said sitting up. "It would serve him right after what he did to me the other day."

"It was unforgivable," Liza agreed, reaching both hands into the rippling water and splashing her face. "Showing off his body like that, just to distract all the women in the audience."

"Exactly," Lauren said, pulling her T-shirt over her knees. "He didn't fight clean. A debate should be a war of words, not a striptease. I'm going to get him back for humiliating me in front of all those people."

"What are you going to do?" Faith asked. "Do you have a plan?"

"Not yet. But now that we've both turned in our articles on the locker room story, I have some free time to think about it. In fact, that's all I'm going to think about until the awards banquet tomorrow night."

"Maybe you could dump something rich and gooey all over his tuxedo," Lisa suggested.

"Dash wouldn't wear a tuxedo, even for this," Lauren said, resting her chin on her knees. "Besides, that wouldn't cut deep enough. It has to be something that's going to make him feel as small and insignificant as he made me feel. Something that will make him regret the day he ever called me helpless."

"I wish I could be there to see it," Liza said, dipping her feet in the water. "You sure you can't get me a ticket to this banquet? I have a great sequinned dress I can wear."

"Sorry," Lauren said, "but it's mostly faculty. The only students invited are the ones being honored."

"Well, I'll be there in spirit," Liza said. "If you start to lose your nerve, just think of me cheering you on."

"I will," Lauren said with a warm smile. "You've already been such a big help."

"So many problems!" Melissa said, sliding off the raft into the water. She ducked beneath the surface for a moment, and reemerged, her hair slicked straight back. "How about you, Faith? What are you worried about?"

Faith ran her hands through her long hair, which was on its way back to blond since most of the brown rinse had washed out. "Well, I'm not *worried* exactly," she said, "but I'm incredibly excited about tomorrow night."

"She's meeting Scott at The Pub," Liza told Melissa.

"For a *drink*," Lauren emphasized.

"Winnie told me about your fake ID," Melissa said. "Just be careful. You don't want to get caught."

"And don't go overboard with the alcohol," Lauren added. "Remember, this is your first drink. You have no idea how it will affect you."

"Would everyone please stop treating me like a baby?" Faith begged. "I can handle myself, okay?"

"Yeah, leave her alone," Liza said, coming to her rescue. "Faith's a big girl. Besides, I'll be with her the entire time." Liza winked broadly. "When I'm not with Jason, that is."

Faith gave Liza a grateful look. Liza was the only one of her friends who truly understood that she needed to be carefree and fun-loving. Why hadn't Faith realized that before? Faith was beginning to regret all the months she'd been so cold to Liza, but she could start making up for it now.

"Are you planning to bring Jason to the snatch breakfast on Sunday?" Faith asked, giving Liza's hand a squeeze. "I'm going to bring Scott if things go well tomorrow night."

"Absolutely," Liza said. "First thing Sunday, I'm going to wake him up with my rousing rendition of 'Oh, What a Beautiful Morning,' then I'm going to haul him into the dining commons. It's going to be great. We'll probably end up spending the rest of the day together."

"Wow, Liza," Faith said, "just listening to you makes me feel like I can do anything."

"You can!" Liza assured her. "You just have to know what you want."

While her friends were lounging on the raft, KC was opening her mailbox in the lobby of her dorm.

Please let there be a check from Grandma Rose, KC prayed as she removed the thick stack of magazines and envelopes. KC's grandmother had promised to send her a check to cover this month's Tri Beta dues, and it still hadn't arrived.

KC looked at her gold antique watch, another

gift from Grandma Rose. She only had ten minutes to get all the way across campus to her Intro to Business class. She'd have to wait until she got there before she could go through the pile.

Tossing the mail into her briefcase, KC pushed open the front door to Langston House and stepped smartly across the green. It didn't matter that she felt like dragging her feet, felt like crawling back into bed, as she had ever since she'd found that letter in Peter's room. Appearances were all she had left. Her life might be falling apart, but at least she could still look good.

"Want a ride?" asked a cute guy on a bicycle, whom KC had never seen before.

KC shook her head and continued toward McLaren Plaza. She knew she looked crisp and cool in her sleeveless white linen dress, a recent purchase with the leftover money from her modeling shoot for *Western* magazine. Her hair was freshly washed and her makeup had been deftly applied, using a few tricks some of the other models had taught her.

"Hi there!" said a handsome guy in shorts, crossing in front of her. "What's your name?"

KC didn't bother to answer. It didn't make her feel any better that guys noticed her everywhere she went. Her whole soul ached with a single word: *Why?* Why had Peter betrayed her? Why, after all the time they'd spent getting to know each other, after all the problems they'd overcome, was he so willing to throw it all away? Hadn't she meant anything to him?

KC had lain awake the past two nights, asking herself these questions over and over again. Had she done something to drive him away? Had she misjudged him? Was his sincerity and lack of pretension just an act? Had she just been a fling for him while he was waiting for his ticket to Europe?

KC reached the cobbled bricks of McLaren Plaza and walked beneath the cherry trees toward Lindsey Chitterton Hall. How long were these same questions going to play themselves in her mind? KC hurried up the steps of the old granite building and into the high-ceilinged hall. Her business class started in two minutes. KC hoped it would be an interesting topic, like mergers and acquisitions, to help take her mind off Peter.

"KC!"

KC turned around. Peter was running down the hall toward her, his sneakers squeaking against the marble floor. His face was flushed, his T-shirt was sticking to his damp skin, and he seemed out of breath. But to KC, he'd never looked more attractive. KC felt an overwhelming urge to throw her arms around him, not even caring if his sweat ruined her brand new dress.

But that would be a big mistake. Peter had betrayed her. He'd lured her into a false feeling of safety, made her think it was okay to tell him the most intimate, private, personal thing she'd ever said to anyone. Then he'd proven that he'd never really cared about her in the first place.

KC tried to set her face into an expression of stony immobility, but she had a feeling it wasn't working. "Hello, Peter," she said, hurt and resentment creeping into her voice.

"Do you have a minute?" he asked. "I really need to talk to you."

"Sorry," KC said stiffly, "but I've got class now." Brushing past him, she headed down the hall.

"I know," he said. "That's why I'm here. I mean, I knew you'd be here and I wanted to catch you before you went in. I've just made a big decision, and I wanted to tell you about it."

"There's no need to include me in any of your decisions," KC said, finally managing the cool tone she'd attempted before. "What you do with your life is none of my business. You made that very clear the other day."

KC tried to enter the open door of the classroom, but Peter blocked her path. "*Listen* to me!" he begged. "I'll make it quick."

There were dark circles under his eyes, and his face looked gaunt and tired. He didn't *look* like the kind of guy who would lead a woman on. He looked like the Peter she'd thought she knew. The Peter who never said something unless he meant it.

KC checked her watch. "You have thirty seconds."

"Fine. First of all, I want you to know that I haven't slept the past two nights because I feel so terrible about what happened. I never meant to deceive you or hurt you in any way. I just figured there was no point telling you about the photo competition since I probably wasn't going to win anyway."

"Uh huh . . ." The words sounded right, but KC had been fooled before. Why should she believe he was telling the truth this time?

"I did send in my final application for the contest," Peter continued, "but I've thought about it a lot since then. I've decided that even if I do win, I'm not going."

"You're not?" KC asked. "Why not? That letter said it was some big, prestigious thing."

"Isn't it obvious?" Peter asked, gripping her bare shoulders. His brown eyes were filled with pain. "I couldn't possibly leave you. I love you!"

"You what?" KC asked, her mouth dropping open. After all the agony she'd suffered the past two days, this was the last thing she'd expected to hear. Or maybe she hadn't heard it at all. She hadn't slept either in the past two days. Her mind had to be playing tricks on her.

"I love you, KC," Peter said again, drawing her closer.

KC burst into tears. "No, you don't," she sobbed. "I know you're lying. Or maybe I'm dreaming. Or maybe . . ."

Peter wrapped his arms around her and kissed her fiercely on the mouth. KC's head began to spin, and she collapsed in his arms. This had to be a dream. Any minute she was going to wake up in her narrow bed and feel as alone as before.

"Are you in or out?" asked the nasal voice of Naomi Potemkin, the graduate student who taught KC's Intro to Business discussion group. Naomi stood just inside the door, nodding toward the podium where Ms. Malmo, KC's professor, was organizing her notes.

KC looked helplessly at Peter. "I've got to go," she said.

Her head still spinning, she ducked into the classroom, climbed the shallow stairs two at a time and found a seat just as Ms. Malmo began her lecture.

"Today," said Ms. Malmo, a slender woman of around forty, "we will talk about techniques used in market research. Before a manufacturer introduces a new product, he'll test it first, to see how consumers will respond. One of the most important testing techniques is the focus group . . ."

KC knew she should be taking notes, but her mind was still out in the hall by the door. Her lips were quivering, and the tears were running down her face faster than she could wipe them away with her fingers. Her breath came in quivery gasps.

She still couldn't believe what had just happened. How was it possible to be down so low one minute, then the next minute feel like your head was bumping against the ceiling?

Peter loved her! He wasn't abandoning her after all! In fact, he was giving up the biggest opportunity of his life, just to be with her.

KC had read the letter from the Morgan Foundation. Thousands of people applied for this grant, and only a few were chosen. It sounded like an important career move for a photographer, one that would be very difficult for Peter to turn down. Yet he'd do it—for her.

KC leaned back against the hard, wooden chair and sniffled loudly, wishing she'd thought to bring a tissue. This had to be the most important thing that had ever happened to her. No guy had ever said he loved her before. And no one had ever made such a huge sacrifice for her, not even her parents.

"So after a focus group has been selected, a moderator leads them in a discussion, trying to learn how they feel about a particular product while the manufacturer observes, unseen, from behind a two-way mirror," Professor Malmo droned on.

KC couldn't stop the tears from flowing, even though the people around her were looking at her curiously. She felt restless. She wanted to run back down the stairs and go find Peter. She wanted to scream out loud so that everyone in the huge lecture hall could hear. *Peter loves me!* She wanted to rip the pages from her notebook and tear them up into little pieces of confetti.

She certainly wasn't capable of paying attention to the lecture. So reaching down beside her chair, KC quietly unsnapped the lock on her briefcase and reached in for the handful of letters and magazines.

Slipping the pile onto her lap, KC shuffled through it and beamed when she saw the familiar lavender-tinted and lavender-scented envelope of her Grandma Rose's stationery. Dropping the other mail back into her briefcase, KC ran a fingernail under the flap of the envelope and pulled out a lavender sheet of notepaper and a check on yellow safety paper. On the check were the words "two hundred" written in her grandmother's pointy, precise script.

It took every ounce of KC's self control not to break down completely. Two hundred dollars! That would pay her Tri Beta dues for the next four months! KC felt so lucky, so loved. Not only was the most wonderful guy in the world in love with her, she also had the most generous, wonderful grandmother. KC's tears dripped onto the check, causing the "hundred" to run.

Hastily slipping the check into her briefcase, KC made a mental note to call Grandma Rose as soon as she got back from class. Grandma Rose was so great, and so much like her. After Grandpa Charlie had died in his early fifties of a heart attack, Grandma Rose had taken over his plumbing supply business. In a few short years, she'd transformed it from a moderately successful company into a thriving operation, and all this while she was in her fifties. She'd never even gone to business school.

Like KC, Grandma Rose favored expensive, tailored suits and Italian leather handbags and shoes. And unlike KC's hippie parents, Grandma Rose completely understood why it was so important KC join a sorority. It was hard to believe KC and her grandmother had so much in common with each other, and so little in common with KC's father, who was Grandma Rose's son. KC's father was happy running a health food restaurant, where he practically gave the food away. He wasn't interested in making a profit, and cared even less about clothes or making social connections.

Eagerly, KC opened her grandmother's letter:

My darling KC—

Here's another token of affection from your grandmother who loves you so much. Don't you dare tell your father I did this. He'll never forgive me for supporting your "vice," as he calls it. Sometimes I'm convinced they switched babies on me in the hospital when Frankie was born. We never agree on anything.

I learned a very important lesson, though, from all our disagreements. Nothing I said or did was going to change him one bit, so I stopped wasting my breath. And you know what? We get along better now, even if he does think I spend too much money on clothes.

I guess what I'm really trying to do is pass along some grandmotherly wisdom, in the hopes you'll avoid some of the pain I've suffered. If you love someone, you have to let them be themselves and do what they want to do. That's the only way they'll be happy, and they'll love you more for it.

Write if you need more money. It will be our secret.

> *Love and kisses,*
> *Grandma Rose*

KC grew thoughtful as she refolded her grandmother's letter and slipped it back in the envelope. Stuck in her mind was the part about letting the people you love be themselves, and letting them do what they want to do. The more KC thought about it, the more she began to feel she was being very selfish.

Eleven

"**A**re you sure this outfit isn't too risqué?" Faith asked Liza for the fifth time as the two girls strolled down Center Street Saturday night. "I feel so—undressed!"

Faith's ensemble, black stretchy bicycle shorts and a black lacey top that looked more like a brassiere, had come straight out of Winnie's closet. Over it, Faith wore a cropped, red denim jacket decorated with colorful pins and buttons Winnie had collected on her trip through Europe. Only the cowboy boots belonged to Faith. Winnie had insisted they were the perfect complement to Faith's outfit.

"For the fifth time," Liza said patiently, "you look great! Scott's eyes are going to pop out when he sees you." They passed Hondo's Café, home of the foot-long submarine sandwich, a squat, brick restaurant with old-fashioned plate glass windows.

Faith fingered the fake ID in her pocket, hard and smooth like a credit card. It felt deceptively innocent, just a little piece of plastic. Yet she had about as much right to carry it as she did stolen money, and it could get her in just as much trouble.

Despite her best efforts at playing the role of the new carefree, fun-loving Faith, she hadn't been able to resist the temptation to sneak over to the law library and look up the local statutes for alcohol-related offenses. Her heart had nearly stopped cold when she'd learned that obtaining alcohol illegally was a felony. If she got caught, she could even serve time in jail!

Faith had been tempted to run back to her dorm and cut the ID into tiny pieces. But she'd stopped herself, just in time. If she chickened out now, her life would never change.

What it all boiled down to, Faith realized, was growing up. She couldn't stay a kid forever, safe and warm in her jammies on a Saturday night. Sure, some of it sounded scary, but the danger was what made it so exciting.

Besides, Faith wouldn't be going through this alone. She had Liza and Scott to guide her through.

"How do I look?" Liza asked, pausing before a darkened store window to look at her reflection.

"You look great!" Faith said, overstating the truth a little. Actually, Liza looked like she was popping out of a lowcut, purple minidress that seemed two sizes too small. Liza's chubby thighs bulged through the diamond shaped holes of her black fishnet stockings and she wobbled precariously in black, high-heeled pumps. Liza's wildly frizzy hair, recently re-dyed, glowed an almost radioactive orange.

"Thanks," Liza said. "This is the night I make my big play for Jason, unless he comes after me first." She wiggled her dark brown eyebrows and her bright red lips curled upwards into a knowing smile. "In this dress, I don't think I'll have to try too hard."

Even without the thumping bass line of loud rock music, Faith would have known they were nearing The Pub. In fact, the bar seemed to have turned inside out since last Saturday night. Dozens of raucous jocks had spilled out onto the sidewalk in front of the small, white-shingled building. They were laughing, drinking, and shouting themselves hoarse, celebrating the eighteenth straight victory of the U. of S. volleyball team.

"Oh boy," Faith said uncertainly as they pushed through the crowd, trying to find the door. "I'll be lucky if I can even find Scott."

"Oooh baby!" shouted a loud male voice from somewhere up above Faith. "That's a hot little cowboy outfit!"

Faith self-consciously pulled her jacket tighter over her skimpy top and plowed through the beefy bodies, finally making her way into The Pub. The place was so jammed, though, it was impossible to see more than a few feet ahead of her.

"I'm going to try to find Jason!" Liza shouted over the music. "I'll catch up with you later."

Faith nodded and, on a hunch, tried to push her way toward the pool table in the middle of the room. Already sweating from the combined temperature of so many bodies crushed together, Faith finally spotted Scott's blond head bent over a pool cue.

As Faith burst from the crowd, Scott happened to look up, and the pool cue leapt from his fingers, sending the white ball skidding into a corner pocket.

"You lose!" one of his friends cried exultantly. "Finally!"

"No fair," Scott protested. "I was distracted." He gave Faith a long, lingering look that sent a shiver down her back. Faith casually let go of her jacket so it fell open. "Forget it!" Scott said to his friends, falling flat on the pool table in a mock faint. "You can keep the money. I've got better things to think about." Crawling across the pool table toward Faith, he raised himself up onto a handstand and flipped over backward, ending up a few inches away from her.

"Hi," Faith said, gazing steadily into his eyes. Just being near him made her heart race. She felt nervous and giddy, and her skin felt hot and flushed.

"That's an incredible outfit," Scott said in a husky voice. "And your hair looks nice, too." He picked up a strand of her honeyblond hair. "Did you dye it back again?"

"No," Faith said. "The brown rinse washed out."

Scott stroked her hair, and Faith felt like melting. "Well, you're just as beautiful blond as you are brunette," he said. "I'm glad you made it over here tonight."

"Me, too," Faith said softly. Though the bar was jam packed with people, it felt like Scott was the only other person in the room. Faith had to laugh at the fears she'd had. This wasn't scary. This was great!

"Hey, Scott!" called one of his friends from the pool table. "Want me to rack up another game?"

"No thanks," Scott said, draping an arm over Faith's shoulder. "Faith and I have some important matters to discuss."

"We do?" Faith asked, as he led her toward a side wall where there was a bank of pinball machines. Then she realized how naive that sounded. Scott was just trying to spend some time alone with her, if you could call being crammed into a room with three-hundred other people "alone." Scott loaded two quarters in the slot of a pinball machine called Joyride, which featured a racy illustration of a biker gang on motorcycles.

"You go first," he said, stepping aside so Faith could start.

"I'm not very good at this," she warned him as she took her place at the flipper buttons. "You'll win easily."

"Who said this was a competition?" Scott asked, moving in behind her and placing his hands over hers.

Faith's heart jumped as Scott's chest pressed against her back. His body felt so warm, so protecting. Faith closed her eyes and leaned against him, feeling his hair brush against her face. Then she felt the softness of his lips brush against her cheek.

"How do you like the game so far?" Scott asked.

"I would say we're both winning," she answered.

Scott wrapped his arms around her and squeezed her tight. Then he tickled her bare stomach.

"Hey!" Faith cried, giggling. "Stop that!"

"I couldn't resist," Scott said. "I had to find out if

you're ticklish."

"Well, now you know!" Faith protested, trying to shield her stomach with her arms.

Scott stopped tickling her, but he grabbed her around the waist and lifted her up off the floor. Then he started pushing his way through the crowd.

"Where are we going?" Faith asked, still giggling.

"For a drink," Scott said, shifting her up a little in his strong arms.

Faith gulped. She'd been having such a good time, she'd almost forgotten about her fake ID. Suddenly, she wasn't sure she had the nerve to use it.

"Uh . . . I don't know," Faith said. "I'm not really that thirsty, yet."

"Oh, come on. You've got to try out your new ID sooner or later," Scott said, placing her on her feet near the bar. He flagged the bartender over. "I'll have whatever's on tap," he said, flashing his fake driver's license. "How 'bout you, Faith?"

With Scott smiling so warmly and the bartender looking so harried and impatient, Faith felt cornered. Everything was going so well. For the past few minutes, she hadn't felt like she was playing a part at all. For those few minutes, she'd actually *been* the girl she'd only pretended to be before. She couldn't back down now.

"I'll have what he's having," Faith said weakly.

"Let me see your ID," said the bartender, a pasty-faced young man whose long, dark hair was pulled back in a ponytail.

Faith fished around in the pocket of her denim jacket and pulled out the plastic laminated card identifying her as Cheryl White. Letting it drop on the counter, Faith held her breath as the bartender studied it. He glanced up at her, then down at the card, a frown on his face. *Stay cool,* Faith warned herself. *If you look nervous, he'll get suspicious.*

The next thing Faith knew, the bartender had disappeared. He was back a few seconds later with two frosty glass mugs. "Three dollars," he told Scott.

Faith let out a deep sigh of relief as the bartender scooted away to help the rest of the clamoring customers.

Scott handed Faith her mug. "Just doing our civic duty, right Cheryl?"

Faith grinned. "Right."

"I'd like to propose a toast," Scott said, lifting his own mug from the wooden bar, which was wet with spilled beer. "To blonds, brunettes, and pretty cowgirls in short red jackets."

Faith clinked her glass against his, then watched him take a long swig of beer.

"Well?" Scott asked, nodding toward her mug.

It was time. Faith had to let Scott see how

sophisticated she was, how taking a drink was no big deal. If she hesitated too long, or acted scared, he'd realize she'd just been faking it up 'til now.

Though Faith felt like she was pretending again, she raised the cold glass with its U of S logo, and grinned confidently.

"Now it's my turn to propose a toast," she said. "To eighteen wins in a row, to poolsharks, and to living life one day at a time!"

"Here here!" Scott said, clinking glasses with her again.

Faith pressed the cold glass to her lips and tilted her head way back, letting the foamy brew run down her throat. She forced herself to swallow, but she really wanted to gag. The stuff tasted like moldy cardboard and smelled like warm sweat. But at least she'd managed to drink it. That was something to celebrate.

Faith came up for air and wiped off the foam that had settled on her upper lip. "Good stuff!" she said, hoping that was an appropriate remark.

"Chug-a-lug!" Scott said appreciatively. "Looks like you know how to put it away."

The worst was over. He'd bought her performance. Now all Faith had to do was give him more of the same. Faith took a second swallow of beer, which wasn't as bad as the first. The beer didn't taste any better, but at least she knew what to expect. She was also beginning to feel even warmer than she had before. Faith took off her jacket and Scott stared appreciatively as her bare arms and midriff came into view.

"Let me take that off your hands," he said, draping the jacket over the back of a nearby chair.

"Thanks," Faith said, taking another sip of beer. She was starting to relax again. She didn't even feel embarrassed at being so uncovered. Maybe it was because Scott had been so complimentary, or maybe she was just getting used to her new image. After Faith had drained the tall glass, she stopped worrying about what she was wearing. She was having too much fun.

A new song came on the stereo, with a catchy, funky beat. It was time to enter stage two of her personality makeover. It was time to dance. "This is a great song!" Faith shouted. "We have to dance to this!" Grabbing Scott's hands, she pulled him toward an area of the bar where couples were gyrating.

Faith tried to get into the music. She tapped the toe of her cowboy boot, feeling the rhythm enter her body, making her heart pound in time to the beat. Then she started clapping her hands and shaking her hips.

"Wooo!" Scott shouted, encouraging her.

Faith felt her body loosen up and she tried to forget about the other people on the dance floor.

It didn't matter what they thought of her anyway. Scott was the only one who mattered. And Scott danced with complete abandon, his face glowing with exhilaration.

If Scott could do it, she could, too. Faith flailed her arms and shook her hair and let the music take her over completely. She twirled and stomped her feet, even singing along though she'd never heard the song before. She tried to lose herself completely in the music. She wasn't Faith Crowley any more. She was just heat and motion and arms and legs and hair.

"Excuse me. Excuse me, please," Lauren said that same evening, trying to make her way through the crowded ballroom of the President's Hall. The vast room was a sea of round tables covered with white linen. The black and white of tuxedos was punctuated by flashes of bright blue silk or red taffeta evening gowns.

Lauren wore a modestly-cut, long, black velvet dress with short sleeves and a black satin sash. Her hair was pulled up off her face in a twist, with loose wisps escaping around her face, showing to advantage her single strand of pearls, which KC had finally given back to her after an extended loan.

"Table Six," Lauren said to herself, checking the

cream colored cardboard placecard in her white-gloved hand. She spotted her table near the front of the room, beneath a raised dais on which there was a long table, also covered with a white linen cloth.

Table Six was nearly filled, with only one empty seat—next to Dash.

Even from a distance, the sight of Dash made Lauren's eyes fill with tears. He looked like his usual cocky, confident self in an oversized black tuxedo jacket with a white button down shirt and a bright green bowtie. His dark hair was slicked straight back, showing off his sculpted features.

But Lauren now realized he was just a beautiful, empty shell. The Dash she thought she'd loved, the Dash who supposedly loved her, didn't exist anymore. Or maybe he had never existed in the first place.

The Dash sitting at Table Six only cared about showing the world how clever he was. The only thing he loved was the sound of his own voice. Winning the debate had been so important to him that he was willing to humiliate her, completely unconcerned about her feelings.

As Lauren approached the table, she blinked to clear away the tears. The last thing she wanted was for him to see how much he'd hurt her. There was no way he'd accuse her of being a helpless female again.

No. The thing to do was be tough—strong. If Dash could forget so easily all they'd meant to each other, then so could she.

"Lauren!" Dash greeted her, jumping up to pull out her chair for her.

Lauren noted with scorn that he was wearing black jeans and high-top sneakers. Didn't he have respect for anything? While Lauren wasn't thrilled to be wearing one of her "society" dresses, at least she knew how to dress appropriately for a special occasion.

"You look nice," Dash said, kissing her on the cheek as she sat down.

"Thanks," Lauren said, not returning the kiss or the compliment.

"You excited about the award, fellow journalist?" he asked.

Lauren gave him a cold look. Dash was even more callous than she'd thought. Not only had he tortured her in front of hundreds of people, but now he was acting like everything was fine between them. Didn't he feel the slightest bit sorry for what he'd done?

"Dash Ramirez!" said a tall, slender woman in her mid-twenties, rushing over to their table. "I heard about your award, and I just had to congratulate you."

"Thanks," Dash said. He turned to Lauren. "This is Alyse Walker, the teaching assistant from my journalism class."

"I read your article on the hazing incident," Alyse went on, "and I was very impressed. In fact, I was so impressed, I showed it to Professor Van Westering. He teaches at the grad school. I thought he should know about you. He's got contacts at journalism schools all over the country."

Dash doled out one of his sexy grins. "Thanks," he said. "I'll need all the help I can get."

Lauren looked from Dash to his T.A. in disbelief. Was Dash just going to sit there and soak up the credit for the article without even introducing her?

"Dash!" said a dark-haired man with a thick moustache, approaching their table.

"Professor Garcia!" Dash said. "What are you doing here?"

"I was on the Regents board this year," Professor Garcia said. "And I want you to know how impressed we all were with your effort. Truly, a professional piece of writing. You must have learned it from me, eh?"

Dash turned to Lauren. "Professor Garcia taught my English section last year. Taught me everything I know."

Lauren was beginning to feel like she was invisible. As far as these people were concerned, Dash had written the article all by himself.

"So tell me, Dash," Alyse asked, "how did you manage to find out about the fraternity hazing before it happened?"

"Well, I didn't do it alone," Dash finally admitted. "Lauren Turnbell-Smythe, here, worked right alongside me. You might say we had an inside tip that there was going to be some trouble, so we made sure we'd be in the right place at the right time."

We? The tears Lauren had been trying so hard to suppress, sprung to her eyes again. This was the cruelest blow of all. Dash hadn't been anywhere near when the ODT's were locking Howard in the trunk of the car. And it had been Lauren who'd gotten the tip from KC.

"It's good you had some help," Professor Garcia said, with a nod to Lauren. "I always like to have someone take a look at my articles before they're published. It gives you a fresh perspective on your work."

"Two heads are better than one," Dash agreed, his face tilted up to his professor's.

Lauren wanted to scream. Everyone was talking about her like she had merely edited Dash's work. Even worse, Dash was doing nothing to dispel this illusion. Lauren hadn't believed she could be angrier at Dash than she'd been the other day, when he'd pulled his stunt at the student union. But now she felt her chest heaving in rage beneath the black velvet.

Lauren wanted to break the gold-trimmed

president's china over Dash's head. Or maybe she could stab him with a sterling silver fork or strangle him with her pearls. She had to do something to get him back, but she knew violence wouldn't work. She'd get in too much trouble. Besides, something more subtle was in order.

Then it hit her. She was in a perfect position to deliver a single, decisive blow more painful than any physical injury she could inflict. More painful, and more lasting.

"Having a good time?" Dash asked, placing a friendly hand on the back of her chair.

"Wonderful," Lauren said with a smile, delicately removing her dainty, white gloves.

Twelve

"Excuse me!" Liza bawled in her brassy voice, trying unsuccessfully to squeeze between two jocks whose backs were pressed together.

Liza had been trapped by an unyielding wall of bodies for the past five minutes, and she was beginning to fear her air supply was running out.

"I said *excuse me!*" Liza repeated, "accidentally" stepping on a sneakered foot with the spikey heel of her right pump.

"Aaagh!" the owner of the sneaker yelled, jerking his knee up to grab his skewered foot.

Liza took advantage of the shift in weight to

dodge through the small opening it created. This brought her one foot closer to Jason, who stood with a group of guys near the giant television screen on the other side of the pool table. They were talking and laughing and having a great time, and Liza wanted to be part of it.

"Jason!" Liza called, trying to make herself heard over the loud music, but she was still too far away.

The pool table still stood between them, not to mention a few dozen football, basketball, and volleyball players. There was a billiards game in progress, the colored and striped balls momentarily still on the green felt surface. A player was chalking up his cue and surveying the balls with a professional air. Liza, too, sized up the table for her next move.

"Excuse me!" she shouted, hoisting herself up onto the pool table and gingerly stepping around the balls, careful not to disturb them.

"Hey!" someone called out. "What do you think you're doing?"

"Shortcut!" Liza said brightly, wiggling her tush as she hobbled across the table and lowered herself down on the other side. Though the pool players were giving her dirty looks, Liza was very proud of herself. She'd cut at least fifteen minutes off her travel time across the bar. Jason was now within striking distance.

"Jason!" Liza called, reaching up high to wave her red fingernails above the heads of the towering jocks. She could hear his voice now, above the music.

"So then she takes a flying leap onto my lap and lands like a sack of cement. I've got strong legs, but I swear I thought they were going to break under all that weight."

Liza stopped dead in her tracks.

"Then she starts flirting with me," Jason told his friends, "or, at least, that's what she thought she was doing. But it was more like a cartoon." Jason puckered up his lips and rolled his eyes. "I can help your career if you're real nice to me," he said in a brassy voice, rolling his eyes and wiggling his hips. "I wanted to burst out laughing, but I didn't have the heart. She really thought she was sexy! What a joke!"

Jason and his friends guffawed with laughter.

"And you should see her hair!" Jason continued. "I swear it's the color of cheddar cheese. Now you *know* a color like that comes out of a bottle."

"Stop it!" one of Jason's friends begged, clutching his stomach from laughter. "You're killing me!"

Liza was barely breathing. She stared at Jason's laughing profile in shock. While it had taken her a few moments to figure out whom he was talking about, there was no longer any question in her mind. He was talking about her. Liza knew the smart thing would be to leave, but she couldn't get her legs to move. Out of some sort of perverse curiosity, she couldn't leave until she'd heard every nasty word.

"Wait!" Jason sputtered through his own laughter. "Wait 'til you hear about her outfit. She was wearing this tight, stretchy black thing that made her look like a Goodyear tire. Or maybe the Goodyear blimp! I tried to shake her, but she followed me around all night."

"Maybe she couldn't help it," said a tall guy with a blond crewcut. "Maybe she was so in love with you, she couldn't help herself."

"Tell me about it," Jason said. "She was on me like suction cups."

"You great big hunk of manflesh, you!" another guy said in a screechy falsetto, making kissing noises.

Jason and the rest of them roared with laughter. "That sounds just like her!" Jason cried.

Even after the laughter finally subsided, Liza stayed rooted to the spot where she was standing. Her skin felt cold and goosebumps covered her pale flesh. She felt like the world's biggest fool.

How could she have misjudged Jason so completely? He *had* seemed interested in her, hadn't he? Liza had thought she was getting the right signals from him. Then again, she had no way of knowing what the right signals were since she'd never had a real relationship with a guy before. All the things she'd said to Faith and the others about having lived and knowing her way around men were purely wishful thinking.

At the rate she was going, it looked like she never would have any sort of relationship. If all guys reacted to her the way Jason did, then she might as well give up now. She wasn't sexy or mysterious or alluring. She was a pushy, fat, overanxious clown.

Liza felt something cold and wet on her cheek. She realized she was crying. Not wanting Jason to see her, not wanting anyone to see her, Liza self-consciously pulled down the hem of her short dress, and squeezed her way around the pool table.

Liza saw Faith dancing with Scott, her blond hair snapping around her head like a whip. Liza had told Faith that the two of them would leave together, but Faith was having such a good time, Liza didn't want to drag her away. Besides, Faith had Scott. Scott would walk her home.

Ducking her head, Liza pushed her way out the door of The Pub and started her lonely walk back toward the dorms.

"Moving on to the Journalism category," said Professor Garcia, leaning into the microphone on the dais, "the first award is for investigative reporting."

Lauren, who'd been sipping water from a crystal goblet, nearly spilled it down the front of her dress. The moment she'd been waiting for all night had finally arrived.

Professor Garcia's eyes roamed the large hall until they came to rest on Dash's face. "It is my great pleasure to announce that one of the winners of this award is a former student of mine, Dash Ramirez, ably assisted, I'm sure, by Miss Lauren Turnbell-Smythe."

The audience broke into polite applause and Professor Garcia held up the golden statue. "Would one of you like to come up and say a few words?"

Dash started to rise from his chair, but Lauren swiftly laid a hand on his arm. For once in her life, she was going to speak for herself, and Dash wasn't going to stop her. All night, as she'd sat through the endless dinner and ceremony, she'd practiced what she was going to say over and over in her head until she knew it by heart.

And for once, she wasn't afraid. She was so filled with anger there wasn't room inside her for any other feeling.

"I'd like to accept the award, if you don't mind," Lauren said, quickly rising to her feet.

Dash looked surprised, and a little disappointed. "Are you sure? I mean, I know how uncomfortable you are with public speaking."

He was trying to steal her thunder again, even after everything that had happened. But this time, Lauren wasn't going to let him get away with it.

"How gallant of you to come to my rescue," Lauren said, straightening the sash on her dress. "But I'll be just fine."

Her heart pounding, Lauren threaded her way through the tables toward the stairs leading up to the podium. Now that she'd committed herself, there was no turning back. Dash had been right. She couldn't cry and ask for his help, then expect to be treated as his equal.

Doggedly climbing the stairs, Liza approached Professor Garcia. He extended his broad hand for her to shake. "Doing the honors, eh?" he asked. "Congratulations."

Lauren shook the professor's hand and accepted the gold statue, noting that Dash's name was carved above hers on the base. Then she turned to the army of faces staring up at her intently. For a brief, panic-stricken moment, Lauren felt like she was back at the student union, gazing with horror at hundreds of laughing mouths and mocking eyes. Her body tensed and she clutched the microphone for support.

Then, taking a deep breath, she stared straight ahead of her. "I'd like to thank the Board of Regents for this great honor," she said, trying to project her voice. "Working as a reporter at the

U of S *Weekly Journal*, I've learned a lot more than how to write a good story. I've learned how the world works. I've learned about the ugly side to human nature."

Lauren looked down at Dash, to see if her barb had struck. She seemed to have missed. He was totally engrossed in her speech, and he was smiling.

It was time to bring out the heavy artillery.

"I'd like to thank my partner, Dash Ramirez, for his able assistance in the investigation of my fraternity hazing article," Lauren continued. "When I say 'my', I don't mean to suggest that I did the entire piece by myself. In fact, initially, the idea was his. But *I* was the one who made the initial contacts within the fraternity organizations and it was *my* source who provided the critical information about the hazing of Howard Benmann."

That seemed to hit home. The smile had left Dash's face, and he shifted uncomfortably in his chair.

"Of course, I *tried* to share this information with my partner, but he was nowhere to be found. Long after Dash had given up on the story and gone home, *I* was the one who hid in the bushes near fraternity row. *I* was the one waiting for the frat boys to lock the victim in the trunk of his car. And *I* was the one who scared them away and rescued poor Howard."

The ballroom was utterly silent. The dozens of faces nearest Lauren looked at her with courtesy and respect. All except one.

Dash's eyes were glowing like hot coals, and he was loosening his tie, as if he was getting ready for a fight.

Too late, Dash, Lauren thought, smiling triumphantly. *The fight's almost over. And this time, I'm going to win.*

"The reason I'm telling you this," Lauren continued, "is to prove a point. Too often, when men and women work together, people simply assume that it was the man who did the work while the woman just provided moral support. But I'm not saying this to be critical of men. I'm saying it because I'm jealous!"

There were a few knowing chuckles from the audience, and Lauren knew she'd struck a chord. She didn't even bother to look at Dash anymore. She wanted to enjoy this last moment in the spotlight.

"How nice it must be to get all the credit, even though a woman's done all the work," Lauren said, affecting Dash's nonchalant tone. "How nice to have people assume you're more competent and knowledgeable, merely because you have certain *anatomical differences.*"

Staring down at the raptly attentive faces,

Lauren felt the exhilarating sense of her own power. This must have been how Dash had felt on Wednesday as he controlled the audience's thoughts and emotions through the cleverness of his words.

"I don't place the blame on any one individual," Lauren said, purposely not looking in Dash's direction, "but on society. Throughout history, men have controlled the events, and the way these events have been reported. But that's my point. It's always been *his*-story. It's time we women take the stand and let people know that it was *our* story, too. Thank you."

The whole room burst into thunderous applause, and a few women in the audience cheered. A female professor on the dais said "nice job," as Lauren passed by her.

Lauren smiled. She felt like the applause was carrying her down the stairs.

"You said it!" another woman shouted as Lauren skimmed the floor, heading back to her table.

Lauren nodded, but she wasn't really listening any more to all the adulation. For the first time in days, she felt peaceful and quiet inside. She was even ready to forgive Dash for his stunt at the debate. Maybe that was what it meant to feel self-confident enough so that nothing other people did could bother you.

"Here," Lauren said, placing the award on the

table in front of Dash. "Share the glory."

Dash barely even glanced at the award. His dark eyes became riveted to hers, and Lauren felt like the fury and humiliation she saw there was burning a hole through her head.

"Okay, Dash," she said, trying to make peace, "I know you're upset, but now we're even. Let's just forget about the whole thing, okay?"

Dash didn't answer.

"Dash?"

With his eyes still boring twin tunnels through her skull, Dash pushed back his chair and stood up. Then, without a word, he turned on his sneakered feet and rapidly strode out of the banquet hall.

Thirteen

Five songs later, Faith was exhausted and dripping with sweat. Her muscles felt warm and tingly from her energetic dancing and her hair felt hot on her neck. Twisting her hair into a long coil, Faith held it on top of her head and fanned herself with her hand.

"Had enough?" Scott asked. He'd removed his sweat-drenched T-shirt, and his tan, muscular chest gleamed like a suit of armor. "You're some dancer, you know that? You're wearing me out!"

"I'm dying of thirst," Faith said. "I think I'll get another beer."

The words came out effortlessly, as if she said them all the time. Faith couldn't even remember what she'd been so nervous about before coming here. Drinking was no big deal. Dancing was no big deal. She didn't even feel as if her life had changed drastically.

She did feel diffcrent, though. A little dizzy, and silly, like any minute she might erupt into giggles.

"You want a beer? This round is on me," Faith said, letting her hair fall back down.

"Sure. I'll meet you by the bar," Scott said. "I've got to make a pit stop first."

"Okay. Don't take too long." Faith confidently pushed large athletes out of the way as she made her way to the bar. The Pub was slightly less crowded than it had been earlier in the evening, and she found an empty barstool. Hopping onto it, she waved her hand to flag down the bartender. "Yoo hoo!" she called. "Drought emergency!" Then she laughed at her own joke.

"May I help you?" asked the bartender. It was a different one from the guy who'd served her earlier. This one was older, with a very visible bald spot in the middle of his graying hair.

"Gimme two of whatever's on tap," Faith said confidently.

"Let me see your ID," the bartender said.

"Whatever you say," Faith answered. She pulled her Cheryl White ID out of the pocket of Winnie's jacket and placed it in the bartender's hand.

The bartender looked at the ID for what seemed like a long time. Then he held it up to a light above the bar and studied it even more closely. After another minute, he lowered the card and looked at Faith. Then he looked back at the ID, then at Faith again.

"You do something to your hair?" he asked.

The air suddenly felt very cold on Faith's bare back as the sweat evaporated. Faith's heart started to hammer in her chest, and she was finding it difficult to breathe. "Uh . . . yeah," she said, trying to sound offhand. "I dyed it blond. Blonds have more fun, you know."

"Uh huh." The bartender studied the ID card again. "So when did you say your birthday was, *Cheryl?*"

Even though Faith had practiced the answer for days, she was finding it difficult to think clearly. She was feeling so anxious, she wasn't sure if she could have told him her own birthday. But she had to say something, or she'd give herself away. "October eleventh?" Faith guessed.

"You don't sound too sure about that," the bartender said. "Let me see another piece of identification."

Faith began to panic. This guy was onto her, and there was nothing she could do to save herself. She didn't have another piece of ID with the name Cheryl White. Liza had given the other card back to Cheryl. She was trapped.

"Well?" the bartender asked.

Trying to buy some time to think, Faith pulled out her wallet and riffled through it, pretending to look for what she knew wasn't there. If only Scott or Liza would come by right now and save her. One of them would know what to do.

Faith looked around, but she didn't see either one of them. The bartender was looking at her like she was some sort of criminal which, in a way, she was. Faith had to do something, say something. "Uh . . . I guess I left it at home," she said feebly. "But that's okay. Suddenly, I don't feel very thirsty."

She leaned forward to hop off the barstool, but the bartender's fingers clamped around her wrist. "Just a moment," he said, nodding toward the other end of the bar. A clean-cut young man started walking toward them. As he approached, Faith noticed a logo on the front of his navy blue blazer. The logo said Campus Security.

Faith watched, in growing horror, as the bartender took her fake ID and handed it to the security man. This couldn't be happening. Not to her.

"Come with me, please," the security man said.

"Where?" Faith asked fearfully. To jail? She'd just committed a felony. Was he going to put her in handcuffs and cart her away like an armed robber or a murderer? *Please, Scott,* Faith prayed, *please get me out of this!*

To her great relief, Faith spotted Scott as he made his way toward her. "Scott!" she cried out to him. "I need you!"

"Hi, my beautiful dancing fool," Scott said, slipping his arm around her waist. "Did you buy another round?"

"Not exactly."

"You out of money?" Scott asked, pulling his wallet out of the pocket of his jeans.

"No," Faith said, clearing her throat, and nodding her head toward the security man.

Scott finally caught on and noticed the man in the blue blazer. "Who's this?" he started to say, until his eye fell upon the security logo. "Uh, Faith," he said, without missing a beat, "I just came over here to tell you that I've got to be heading back to campus. We've got an early practice tomorrow morning, and I really need my sleep. I'll call you, okay?" Before Faith could say a word, Scott had literally vanished into the crowd.

Faith was stunned. How could he leave her at a time when she desperately needed help, advice, a familiar face?

Faith stood up on the metal rungs of a barstool and searched for Liza. Liza was her only remaining hope, and Liza had said she would stick by Faith for the entire evening. So where was she? Even in this crowd, Liza's hair would be easy to spot.

But it soon became clear that Faith was alone. She had been utterly abandoned by two people she had thought she could trust. Abandoned at the worst possible moment of her life.

The security man unhooked a large, leather bound notepad from his belt. "Name?" he asked, pulling a pen from the pocket of his blazer and propping the notepad against the bar.

They were going to catch her sooner or later. She might as well tell them the truth. "Faith Crowley."

The man wrote down her name, then took her dorm room number and phone number. "You realize that using false identification to illegally obtain alcoholic beverages is a violation of federal law, as well as university regulations?"

"Yes." Faith hung her head and felt the tears welling in her eyes. "Am I going to jail?"

The man shook his head. "Not exactly."

Before Faith could feel any relief, the man ripped a piece of thin white paper off the top of his pad.

"I'm issuing you a citation," he said. "That means you are officially on probation. If you're caught again, or if you receive one more citation for any offense, you can be expelled. Meanwhile, you'll be called before a U of S peer review board within the next two weeks. If you plan to make any defense of your actions, you can do so then."

Faith felt hot tears spill over her sweaty cheeks. This was so unfair! All her life, she'd been such a goody goody and the one time that she was acting a little bit wild, she was getting into serious trouble.

"You must leave these premises immediately," the man said. "I'll escort you back to campus to make sure you arrive safely."

"Thank you," Faith whispered, slipping her arms into the red denim jacket and buttoning it all the way up. She not only felt like a criminal, she felt like a cheap hussy.

"Let's go," the man said, gesturing with his hand for her to precede him out the door.

Faith got into the security man's van and was driven, like a prisoner, back to Coleridge Hall.

Hugging her statue, Lauren rushed from the President's Hall. She ran through the chandeliered, marble-floored lobby and out the fifteen-foot high doors into the night.

This was supposed to be her big moment of victory. She'd finally put Dash in his place, held the audience spellbound, and gotten the credit she deserved. Yet all Lauren felt inside was an overwhelming need to find Dash. They'd had fights before, but the look in his eyes told her she'd gone too far.

Lauren had been so intoxicated with the sound of her own words that she'd gotten carried away. She hadn't really meant to make it seem as if Dash hadn't done any work. That wasn't the truth, anyway. But she'd been so angry with him she'd forgotten about the truth. She'd forgotten a lot of things. Like how much they meant to each other.

Lauren had no idea where Dash had gone, but he was bound to end up at his room, sooner or later. The smartest move would be to go there and wait. Even if Lauren had to sit on his doorstep all night in her evening gown, it would be worth it if she could just get him to listen to her apology. He'd be sure to forgive her.

Lauren raced across the dorm green toward the dorm parking lot, then across the main street leading into downtown Springfield. While she was nervous about running through the dark streets alone, she was more nervous about somehow missing Dash. Lauren's patent leather pumps barely touched the pavement as she dashed past the chic cafés and pricey boutiques of The Strand, Springfield's fanciest street. Her pace didn't slow as The Strand gave way to a rundown street of vacant lots, abandoned warehouses, and tiny, shabby grocery stores.

The neighborhood improved slightly, giving way to

small brick apartment buildings and dilapidated brownstones. Lauren fell against the stoop of the brownstone where Dash rented his room and tried to catch her breath. Her hair was coming undone, so she quickly pulled out the hairpins and shook it loose. Then, with aching legs, she marched up the steps.

For once, Lauren was glad the front door didn't lock properly. It would give her a chance to get inside Dash's building without his knowing. If he were home and Lauren had asked to be buzzed in, he might have ignored her. Half-dragging herself up the stairwell to Dash's floor, Lauren leaned against his doorbell with all her weight.

"Who is it?" asked a muffled voice from within.

"Dash! It's Lauren!" she cried, still panting.

Dash unlocked the door and opened it, but he didn't invite her in. He simply stood in the doorway with his arms crossed, a scowl disfiguring his handsome face. He was still wearing his black jeans and sneakers, but he now wore an ink-stained, faded, red T-shirt. "What do you want?" he asked.

"I want to talk," Lauren said breathlessly. "I want to explain what happened earlier."

"I think I've heard enough of your speeches for the rest of my life," Dash said.

Lauren searched his eyes for even a hint of warmth or forgiveness, but he looked at her like she was a total stranger.

"Please," she begged. "Just listen to me. I understand why you're angry. I stretched the truth a little bit . . ."

"A little?! It was an outright lie!"

"Okay! I admit it. I made you look bad in front of a lot of people, but that wasn't any worse than what you did to me the other day. I was angry with you. I was just trying to pay you back."

"Well, you did that and more," Dash said, his voice chillingly emotionless. "Consider your account closed." He started to shut the door, but Lauren pushed it open with her hand.

"Don't shut me out!" she begged. "It's over now. Let's call a truce. Let's put this whole thing behind us and forget it ever happened."

"Forget?!" Dash ranted. "Forget that you tried to undermine me in front of the entire journalism department? Forget that you made me look like a liar to the president and provost of the university? I'll never forget this as long as I live! You showed me absolutely no respect."

"Well, what about the way you humiliated me at the debate?" Lauren cried. "What kind of respect were you showing me when you started taking off your clothes?"

"That's not the same thing," Dash argued.

"Of course it's the same thing!"

"I didn't attack you personally," Dash shouted,

pounding his fist against the doorjamb. "I was just trying to be funny. But you were trying to make me look like a lazy, sexist liar who was merely riding your coattails to get this award."

This argument was getting out of control. Lauren had come to apologize, yet things only seemed to be getting worse. Lauren had to try to slow things down.

"I'm sorry if it came across that way . . ." Lauren began.

"It's too late for apologies," Dash cut in. "The damage has been done, and I'll never forgive you for it. I'll never be able to look anyone at the *Journal* in the face after what you did to me tonight, and I certainly never want to see your face again as long as I live."

"Dash!" Lauren cried, unable to believe the cruelty of his words. "You don't really mean that. After you get over your anger, you'll see . . ."

"It's over," Dash said, a look of disgust on his face. "Don't you get it? As far as I'm concerned, you don't exist."

Lauren felt like invisible hands were choking her. Never, in her entire life, had she been treated with such utter contempt. She may have lost Dash, but she couldn't lose the little that was left of her dignity.

"Fine!" Lauren sputtered, managing to hold herself up by clinging to Dash's doorjamb.

This whole encounter still had an air of unreality about it. How could they have gotten to this point so quickly when, just a few short weeks ago, they'd been so in love? This couldn't be happening. Yet Lauren heard the venomous words pour out of her mouth.

"That's just fine with me," she said, her face contorted with rage, "because as far as I'm concerned, you never existed in the first place. I'll put tonight behind me, all right I'll forget I ever even knew anyone named Dash Ramirez!"

Fourteen

....

*E*arly Sunday morning, Melissa was
awakened by the sound of a key
turning in the lock of her dormroom
door. A light sleeper, Melissa opened her eyes at
once and sat straight up in bed. Today was the
snatch breakfast. All over campus, R.A.'s were
unlocking dorm room doors so that the girls
could have free reign to wake up the guy of their
choice.

Melissa focused her eyes on the glowing green
numbers on her digital, bedside clock. It was seven
thirty. Ordinarily, Melissa allowed herself to sleep
in on Sundays, but she had a feeling the dorm was

going to get pretty noisy in a few minutes. Besides, this snatch breakfast would be a good excuse for her to pay Brooks a visit.

Things between them had been tense the past week. They'd never resolved the name issue, and Melissa could tell that Brooks was afraid to bring up the subject. Maybe it was time to soften her stand a little bit.

"Wutamzit?" Winnie mumbled, rolling over onto her side and throwing off the covers.

"Seven thirty," Melissa said, pulling down on the windowshade so that it sprang up, letting in the bright morning light. "Time to snatch your honey out of bed."

"Josh hates getting up early on weekends," Winnie said, flinging her arm over her eyes to block out the light. Then she leapt out of bed. "All the more reason to wake him up as soon as possible."

Kicking aside a colorful pile of dirty lycra running tights on the floor, Winnie headed for her closet. She pulled on a black satin kimono over her paisley print men's boxer shorts and orange T-shirt that said "I'm Still Waiting for the Great Pumpkin." Then she took a bright yellow plastic bucket off her dresser. The bucket was filled with toothpaste, shampoo, cream rinse, and half a dozen small bottles of hair styling lotion. "See you in the bathroom," Winnie called cheerily.

Winnie was always cheerful in the morning. It was one of the few things Melissa hated about her.

After Melissa washed up, she pulled on her regulation gray U of S sweatsuit and running shoes. As Winnie headed down the hall to knock on Josh's door, Melissa began a light jog to Rapids Hall, Brooks's dorm.

Dozens of girls, many fully dressed and made up, were crisscrossing the green, their faces a mixture of hopefulness and anxiety. Melissa still couldn't believe those days of uncertainty were already behind her. She didn't have to worry about getting a date ever again. She had a permanent date for the rest of her life.

Melissa pushed open the back door to Rapids Hall and took the stairs two at a time up to Brooks's floor. A few of the doors were already open. Looking in as she passed, Melissa saw one girl jumping on a guy's bed while he steadfastly tried to sleep, his pillow shielding his head. Melissa reached Brooks's door and gently eased it open.

Brooks's roommate, Barney Sharfenburger, slept soundly, his black, horn-rimmed glasses on the table beside his bed. Brooks, though, was already awake. He lay on his bed, the sheet tucked tightly around his bare chest, staring up at the ceiling. The sunshine danced lightly on his blond curls and classic, well-defined features. Yet, despite his repose, he didn't look happy, and Melissa blamed herself for that.

"Hi," Melissa said softly, not wanting to wake up Barney.

Brooks turned his head on the pillow, and his blue eyes looked almost transparent in the strong light. "I wasn't sure if you were coming," he said.

"Why not?" Melissa asked, stepping over Barney's weight bench but nearly tripping on one of his barbells. She perched on the edge of Brooks's bed and stroked his curls. "There's no one else I'd rather yank out of bed at the crack of dawn."

"That's nice to hear," Brooks said, letting his weighty hand rest on Melissa's leg. "The way you reacted to taking my name, I thought maybe you'd . . ."

"I may not want to take your name," Melissa said, "but that doesn't have anything to do with how I feel about you. I love you. And I know I've been sort of stubborn about this name thing."

"Sort of?" Brooks exclaimed. "That's an understatement."

"You have to understand," Melissa said. "I've always been a loner. I never even had a steady boyfriend, before you, so I never had to think about anybody's needs except my own. But I'm willing to discuss it. Maybe we can come up with some sort of compromise."

"I've been thinking about it, too," Brooks said. "And I had an idea. How about if you call yourself Melissa McDormand-Baldwin? That way you'd have the best of both worlds. You'd keep your name, but people would still know you're married to me!"

"It's not a bad idea," Melissa pointed out, "but that's not a real compromise because you're not giving up anything."

"Me?" Brooks asked, retracting his hand. "What does this have to do with me?"

"I'm not the only one getting married," Melissa said. "If I have to change my name, then you should too. What if we both call ourselves McDormand-Baldwin? That would be truly fair."

Brooks shook his head. "That's too weird," he said. "I mean, I'm sure some guys change their names, but they must be like .00001 percent of the population. Call me old-fashioned, but I don't feel the need to be on the cutting edge of social trends."

"I'm just asking you to make the same sacrifice I'd be making," Melissa said. "But if you can't, then I guess I can't either. I'll just keep the name McDormand."

"Which puts us right back where we started." Brooks pushed himself up to a sitting position and swung his legs around to the floor. He sighed deeply and let his elbows rest on his pajama-covered knees. "What are we going to do?"

"There are only two choices," Melissa said. "Either we both change our names, or neither of us does."

"And that's your final offer?" Brooks looked at her beseechingly, but Melissa was unwilling to budge. Much as she loved him, she could only bend so far.

Brooks seemed to understand this as if she'd said it aloud. "Okay," he said. "You win, my woman warrior. If it's that important to you, I guess I can live with it. The guys at home will think I've lost my mind but, I'll do it. I'll call myself Brooks McDormand-Baldwin."

"What did you say your name was?" the young man asked a slender girl as the two walked past Faith on the dorm green.

"Janet," the girl said, self-consciously wiping at the blush on her cheeks. "I'm in your chemistry section."

"Oh yeah," the guy said, smiling. "You sit four seats to my right."

Faith had witnessed half a dozen conversations like that as she sat alone on the grass, half a dozen beginnings of what could possibly be longterm, happy relationships. Relationships where the girl didn't have to resort to criminal activity to impress the guy, and where the guy wouldn't run out on the girl at the first sign of trouble.

That's what had happened to Faith. She'd figured it out last night as she'd cried herself to sleep, ignoring Liza's demands to know what was wrong. She'd been so infatuated with Scott that she'd been willing to throw away her life, her entire future. What could she possibly have been thinking of when she broke the law? There was nothing exciting or adult about getting arrested. It was just *stupid*.

Faith's stomach had turned to cement at the thought of facing the peer review board. What were they going to do to her? What form of punishment would she get? Would there be spectators at her trial?

The security man had said this would go on her permanent record. Did he mean *police* record? What if she ever tried to get a job in the theater and her employer checked out her background? So much for being a famous and successful director. Faith would be lucky to get any job at all, with a criminal record.

"I'm a felon," Faith told herself. "A convicted criminal."

Faith hugged her legs to her chest and rested her cheek on her knees. She felt like calling her parents and saying "Mommy! Daddy! Come get me! Take me home." But her parents couldn't protect her. If at all possible, she didn't even want her parents to find out about this. The lump in Faith's stomach was churning now.

"Faith!"

Faith felt warm hands on her shoulders, and Scott plopped down on the grass beside her.

"How's it going?" he asked, his tan face relaxed and smiling.

Faith just stared at him, her face a stony mask. He had some nerve even talking to her after abandoning her last night. How could a person be so insensitive?

"Uh oh, don't tell me," Scott said, his brown eyes warm. "They gave you a citation?"

"Don't act all concerned now, after the fact," Faith snapped at him. "The time to act like you cared was last night, when you could have helped me. If there's anything I hate, it's a hypocrite."

"Hey! Hey!" Scott said, reaching for her hands. "Don't be so hard on me."

Faith pulled her hands away and sat on them.

"I had to bail out on you," Scott said, stroking her french braid, "or I would have gotten caught, too. My ID was just as fake as yours."

Faith wrenched her head away from Scott's hand. "So you saved your own skin. That tells me a lot about you."

"Look, I'm sorry. I'm really not a lout," Scott said. "I just couldn't risk getting caught, even for you. If I got a citation, my coach would find out and kick me off the team. I'm on scholarship here."

"Don't expect any sympathy from me," Faith said coldly. "I might get kicked out of school, too."

As Faith stared at Scott's kissable lips, she realized that she'd done it again. She'd let herself be bamboozled by appearances. Scott was just like Christopher Hammond—good looking, charming on the surface, and a slimeball underneath.

Faith stood up. "I wish I could say it's been nice knowing you," she cracked, "but, like I said, I hate hypocrites."

"Hey, wait a minute!" Scott said, leaping up and grabbing her arm. "You're acting like you blame me for what happened to you."

"Very insightful."

"But that's not fair," Scott said, as he kept pace with her rapid strides. "I didn't make you get a fake ID, and it's not my fault if you got caught."

"But you're more experienced at that sort of thing than I am," Faith insisted. "You could have helped me, and you didn't."

"More experienced?" Scott laughed. "You could have fooled me. You were so blasé the day you went to get your ID, I figured it was no big deal for you. And you and your foghorn girlfriend, Liza, barged into The Pub like you'd been there a hundred times before. You're the one who came across as experienced. I figured you could handle the security guy the way you handled everything else."

"Well, you figured wrong," Faith said. "My friend, Liza, may be able to bowl people over with her self-confidence, but I can't. Maybe my mistake was thinking I could be like her."

Or in even listening to her in the first place, Faith thought as she tramped across the grass.

"Faith!" Scott said, laying a hand on her arm. "At least talk to me. I understand, now, why you're angry, but ignoring me won't do any good."

"Oh yes it will," Faith said. "I think ignoring you would be the smartest move, at this point."

"No," Scott argued. "I'm not willing to let this go so easily. I like you, Faith. And I'd like another chance to show you that I'm not the horrible person you think I am."

"Why should I?" Faith demanded. "So you can just leave me in the lurch again? Then I'd feel twice as stupid as I do right now."

"I promise it won't happen again," Scott said. "Please. Just say you'll go out with me sometime. You don't even have to commit to a specific date."

Faith sighed. "I'm sorry, Scott. I just don't feel like taking any more risks."

"It won't be a risk," Scott promised. "Just give me another chance. You'll see."

Faith stopped walking and gazed at Scott's adorable, healthy face. His eyes looked sincere, but she no longer felt like a good judge of character.

On the other hand, Scott was right. He hadn't forced her to get a fake ID, to drink alcohol, or anything else. She'd done it willingly. And what could he really have done to help her? Maybe Faith was blaming Scott when the person she really should be blaming was herself.

"You can have another chance," she said, finally. "But if you really want to keep seeing me, you're going to have to work for it. I'm not feeling too trusting right now."

"Fine!" Scott said. "I want to make this up to you. Whatever it takes, I'll do it."

Fifteen

*L*auren didn't need a mirror to know she looked awful. Her unwashed hair was still stiff with the hairspray she'd used to help keep her hair up, and her eyes were swollen and puffy from a sleepless night spent crying into her pillow.

But her appearance was the last thing on Lauren's mind as she stumbled down the steps to the University Café, making her way blindly in the dim light. The only thing she could think about was that, in just a few seconds, she would have to see Dash again at the *Journal* Sunday breakfast.

Dash! How could she face the rest of her life

without him when she'd barely made it through last night? Her tiny room with its peeling paint, roaches, and leaky plumbing had never seemed so dismal, so depressing, so *scary*. All night she'd heard strange scratching noises and tapping at the window, as if someone was trying to get into her apartment.

Or maybe that was just wishful thinking. No one wanted to get in. She was all alone.

This was much worse than the loneliness she'd felt when she'd first come to U of S That was simply the loneliness of not knowing anyone yet. But at least then she'd had Faith as a roommate and her comfortable room on campus.

Now she didn't even have that. After all the progress she'd made this year, as much as she'd grown, she'd ended up with less than when she started.

"Lauren! Hurry up!" Greg called to her as she emerged from the narrow staircase into the dim, dusty basement café. "We've been waiting for you."

Tired as she was, Lauren's heart jumped at the sight of Dash sitting with the other *Journal* staffers at the long, pushed-together table against the back wall. He looked more unkempt and unshaven than usual. He was wearing the same inkstained red T-shirt from last night, and the same black jeans. In fact, it looked as if he might have slept in them.

Lauren could take no comfort, however, from the fact that Dash looked as bad as she felt. She wanted to hate him. She wanted to find him unattractive. She wanted him to suffer for all the nasty things he'd said to her the night before. But all she could feel was a heaviness, a misery so pervasive it dulled all her sharper emotions.

There was an empty seat next to Dash. Lauren purposely avoided it, taking one across the table and down a few places. It was still too close, though. She could see Dash's bleary eyes and smell the acrid smoke wafting from the cigarette that dangled between his lips. Dash had quit smoking months ago. The fact that he'd started again meant he was taking this even worse than she'd thought.

"Let's get down to business," Greg said, rising from his place at the head of the table. "First off, I'd like to congratulate our Regents winners, Lauren Turnbell-Smythe and Dash Ramirez who received their award last night."

There was polite applause around the table.

"Congratulations," Greg said. "We're very proud of you. I'd also like to report that circulation of this week's *Journal* hit an all-time high, thanks to your article on the locker room issue. I'm sure your debate at the student union really stimulated interest in the story."

"It stimulated a lot more than that," said Ellen

Greenfield, winking at Dash. "You should take your shirt off more often. I'll be happy to interview you."

"Hey!" Charlie Mandelkern said. "You're always yelling at me because *I* sound sexist. You should hear yourself!"

"I think it was an irresponsible act, Dash," said Alison Argonbright, sitting further down the table, near Greg. "Cheap sensationalism at its worst."

"It was brilliant!" Richard Levine argued. "He made his point in a simple, bold, effective manner."

"See what I mean?" Greg said, looking first at Dash, then at Lauren. "Maybe it's just the natural chemistry between you two that makes people take notice but, hey, if it boosts circulation I'm all for it."

Lauren didn't know whether to laugh or cry. Right now the only chemistry between Dash and her was the kind likely to cause a thermonuclear explosion.

"And all this attention has given me a great idea," Greg continued. "Dash and Lauren work so well together, I'd like to make it a permanent thing. I'd like the two of you to write a weekly His-and-Hers column where you'll cover the male and female perspectives on different issues. Maybe I'll even get you to debate each other on a regular basis. It could be great!"

Dash's cigarette fell out of his mouth, causing him to jump up as it singed his jeans. Lauren, who'd been sipping a glass of water, started to choke.

"Whoa!" Greg shouted. "Is something wrong? That wasn't exactly the reaction I expected."

How could Lauren possibly work with Dash again? Every second they spent together would be sheer torture—a reminder of everything they once had and would never have again. But Lauren was a professional. If her editor-in-chief gave her an assignment, she would accept it, no matter how much personal torment it might cause her. Dash, who'd stuck his cigarette back in his mouth, didn't say a word.

"Last chance," Greg said. "If you want to get out of it, say it now."

"You're the boss," Dash said to Greg, though he was glaring at Lauren. "Whatever you say goes."

"Knock, knock," KC said softly, outside the door to Peter's room.

The halls of Coleridge, usually alive with trumpet players or tap dancers or actors practicing their lines, were quiet this morning. Almost everyone on campus was at the dining commons right now, being a snatcher or snatchee.

But KC hadn't come to snatch Peter out of bed. She'd come on a much more serious mission.

For the past two days, KC had read and reread Grandma Rose's letter until the paper had holes in it from the pressure of her fingers. She couldn't stop thinking about what her grandmother had said. *If you love someone, you have to let them be themselves and do what they want to do.* The more KC thought about it, the more she realized her grandmother was right. And the clearer it became what she had to do.

"Peter?" KC called softly.

Hearing no answer from inside Peter's room, KC gently pushed the unlocked door open. Though it was after ten o'clock, Peter was still sleeping. He lay on his back, his chest rising and falling evenly. His hands, roughened from years of dipping them in chemical solutions, were draped placidly across his chest. The wall above his bed was covered with large, glossy black and white photographs, most, KC noticed, featuring her.

KC felt wracked with guilt for ever doubting him. How could she have been so self-centered? She had no right to be angry with him for wanting to go to Europe. Peter had hopes and aspirations just like anyone else. If some of those dreams meant leaving the country, she couldn't blame him for that.

KC knelt by Peter's bed and watched him sleep in the stillness of his room. His hair was all tousled, and he looked so peaceful, so innocent and sweet. She couldn't bear to rouse him from his sleep. Slipping out of her kidskin loafers, KC slipped under the covers with him, her body half-falling out of the narrow bed.

Peter sighed in his sleep and rolled over onto his side, unconsciously making room for KC.

"Peter?" KC whispered, running a finger lightly down the smooth skin of his neck. "Peter, are you awake?"

Peter's eyes opened slowly. He didn't seem startled to see her. He simply draped one of his arms around her and pulled her closer. "Hi," he murmured. "Are you snatching me?"

KC shook her head. "No. I came to tell you something. Something very important."

"Uh oh," Peter said, looking more awake. "Are you still mad at me?"

"What is there to be mad about?" KC whispered, not wanting to break the peace and stillness. "Should I be mad that you love me? Or mad that you're willing to give up the biggest opportunity of your life for me? If there's anyone I should be mad at, it's myself."

"You didn't do anything wrong," Peter said, playing with her hair. "You had a right to be angry."

"Yes, but it was short-sighted of me," KC said. "And selfish. All I could think about was the fact that you'd be leaving me, not how much studying in Europe would mean to you."

"It's okay," Peter comforted her. "I've thought it through, and I'd rather stay here. I couldn't leave you, KC. I'd feel like I'd left part of myself behind."

"Oh, Peter," KC cried, a sob erupting in her throat. "You are so wonderful, you know that? As selfish as I am, that's how good you are. I don't deserve you."

Peter buried his head in her hair. "I'm the one who's undeserving," he whispered. "I feel like the toad that got kissed by the princess, only I'm still a toad and she loves me anyway."

"Don't say that," KC said, her tears wetting the top of Peter's head. "You're always putting yourself down, and there's no reason to. You're handsome, intelligent, sweet, and very, very talented."

"They say love is blind," Peter joked.

"I'm not blind," KC said. "I can see very clearly. And I see that I can't let you give up the Morgan Grant, even if it kills me to be separated from you. Your whole career's at stake. If you win, you have to go."

Peter lifted his head and looked at KC with a mixture of surprise and pain. "No, KC," he said. "We can't go through this again. I've already made up my mind, and I'm happy now."

"But don't you understand?" KC asked, sitting

up straight. "I have to let you go. It's the only way I can prove how much I love you."

"I know you love me," Peter said, pushing himself up so that he was eye level with KC. "I don't need proof."

"But I need to give it to you. And the only way I can be happy is to know I'm making you happy. And to know I'm helping you be everything you want to be. There's no point in arguing with me. I've made up my mind."

Peter's expression softened and he studied her face intently. For several minutes, he didn't say a word.

"Well?" KC asked. "What are you thinking about?"

Peter smiled. "I was just thinking how beautiful you are. And how lucky I was to find someone like you."

"I hope you won't forget me," KC said, "even if you do go away."

"Never!" Peter declared, hugging her tightly. "No matter what happens, we'll figure something out. We love each other. Nothing will ever change that." Then Peter kissed KC with such passion and longing that KC knew there could never be any real distance between them.

Here's a sneak preview of
Freshman Choices, *the fourteenth*
book in the dramatic story of
FRESHMAN DORM.

Scott!" Faith stammered. "What are you doing here?"

Scott Sills didn't answer right away. He looked just as embarrassed as Faith felt. His blond hair was bleached pale by the sun and his face looked just as handsome as ever. It was hard to believe that this was the same person who had left her in the lurch when she'd been caught buying beer with a fake ID.

"What am I doing here?" Scott echoed, his amber eyes flitting about the room full of auditioning thespians. "You know, it's funny, I was asking myself the same thing. I was looking for my touch football game, but I guess I took a wrong turn. Say, why are these people wearing so many clothes? Don't they know it's eighty degrees outside?"

Faith suppressed a smile. "I'm sure they'd be more comfortable if they dressed like you." Wearing only a pair of baggy tropical shorts, Scott stood out from the jacket and tie crowd.

"So how's the volleyball going?" Faith asked, allowing herself a small, artificial smile.

"Great!" Scott said. "We're going to the state finals next week. If we win there, we'll move on to the regionals."

"What's the winning streak up to now?" Faith asked. "Twenty in a row?"

"Twenty-one," Scott said. "It's a new record. I'm going to be in the history books!"

"Pretty impressive."

"Yeah . . ." Scott's eyes flitted around the room again. "So—what *is* this, anyway? A Dress for Success party?"

Faith laughed before she remembered not to. "Sort of," she said. "Everybody's signing up to audition for *Macbeth* or work on the crew. A famous visiting director is in charge, and I think people were expecting to see him today."

"Oh, I get it," Scott said. "This is a Dress to

Impress party."

Faith looked at Scott in appreciation. He was probably the only person in the room who saw things the way she did. But of course, they only saw eye-to-eye on this one point. In every other way, they were incompatible.

Scott was wild and uninhibited. She was practical and steady. He had no goals in life, other than to enjoy himself. She was planning to work hard and make a name for herself in the theater. Besides, he hadn't done anything to redeem himself for abandoning her at The Pub. She had no reason to trust him.

"So . . ." Scott said, shoving his hands in the pockets of his shorts. "I guess you're going to be pretty busy working on this play, huh?"

Faith could see where this was going, but she wasn't sure how to answer. "Well, they're just starting to gear up," Faith said. "The actual work won't start for at least another week."

Scott glanced briefly at Faith's face, then down at the floor. "So does that mean you'll have some free time? To go out with me, that is."

He looked so sad that Faith had a sudden urge to hold him in her arms and run her fingers down his smooth bare back. But that was simply physical attraction, an animal thing that had nothing to do with common sense.

"I'm sorry," Faith said. "But I'm still going to be really busy. I'm planning a big engagement dinner for a friend of mine, and there are a lot of details to think about. I haven't even figured out the menu yet."

"I could help you," Scott offered. "I worked at a couple of different restaurants when I was in high school. I was a waiter, a salad man, a busboy. I could give you *professional* advice. For a small fee, of course." Scott grinned, and Faith found herself grinning back.

"How much?" she asked.

"It's all in the contract," Scott said. "Just don't read the fine print."

Faith was tempted. Compared to these nervous, showy theater majors, Scott was a breath of fresh air. But how could she take him seriously when he walked around half-dressed? No one else seemed to take him seriously, either. People kept staring at him and whispering.

"What part are *you* trying out for?" asked a throaty female voice.

Faith turned. Erin Grant had appeared from the crowd, and she was staring at Scott with disdain. Her long black hair hung to her waist, and her makeup had been carefully applied to emphasize the icy blue of her eyes. She wore a black dress with a handkerchief hemline. No doubt Erin was hoping to win the part of Lady Macbeth, but to Faith she looked more like one of the three witches.

"Oh, wait, I've got it," Erin said. "You're trying out for *Beach Blanket Bingo*, right?"

Scott smiled sweetly. "That would be more up my alley than *Macbeth*."

Erin rolled her eyes. "Seriously. What are you doing here? And by the way, are you aware that there's a university regulation requiring all students to wear both shirts *and* shoes in all public places on campus?"

Scott shrugged. "Sorry."

"Just be glad I'm not your resident adviser," Erin said. With a nasty smile at Faith, she walked away.

"I wish she wasn't *my* R.A.," Faith said, watching Erin add her name to the sign-up sheet. "But that was a good question. What *are* you doing here, Scott?"

"Liza told me where to find you."

"Liza?"

Scott nodded. "I kept waiting to bump into you by accident, but it never happened, so I finally went by your room the other day. Your roommate told me you'd be here at two o'clock."

Faith pressed her lips together and fumed. So that was why Liza had been so insistent that they show up here precisely at two o'clock! And it was typical Scott just to drift for the past two weeks, waiting for fate to bring them together, rather than just call her on the phone like a normal person and arrange a date.

"I'm sorry, Scott," Faith said. "It's not going to work out between us. I need more structure in my life. I like to know in advance when I'm going to see someone. And I also like knowing when someone's going to disappear."

Scott's face fell and, for a moment he didn't say anything. Then he sighed. "Okay," he said. "I don't want to force you into anything. But if you change your mind and want to see me again, give me a call. I'll leave it up to you."

"Bye, Scott," Faith said.

Without another word, Scott padded out of the lounge.

Faith sank into the cushions of the red seating unit and closed her eyes. Why did she feel so sad? Scott wasn't her Mr. Right. She didn't even feel comfortable asking him to help her with Melissa's engagement party. He probably wouldn't show up in the first place. Actually, it would be better if he didn't show up—he was the last person Melissa needed if she wanted an uneventful *sober* party.

This whole thing was Liza's fault. Every bit of it. When would that girl ever learn to stop meddling? Ever since she'd bought Lauren's dorm contract, Liza had been like a splinter under Faith's skin. Everything about her was annoying: her brassy voice, her horsey laugh, the cheap, fruity smell of her perfume, and the shrine of self-portraits that hung above her bed. She was done thinking about Scott Sills until Liza forced him on her again.

How had Faith come to this? Her life had been so calm and predictable when she'd had Lauren for a roommate and Brooks for a boyfriend. But those days were gone forever. The question was, what would take their place next?